Sergios shook his arrogant dark head. "Think outside the box, Beatriz. I'm trying to make a deal with you. As you're not in business, I'll explain—I give you what you want so that you give me what I want. It's that simple—"

"Except when it's my body on the table," Bee replied in a tone of gentle irony. "My body is not going to figure as any part of a deal with you or anybody else. We agreed that this would be a marriage in name only, that there would be no sex, and I want to stick to that."

"That is not the message your body is giving me, *latria mou*," Sergios drawled softly.

Marriage by Command

Three sisters wedlocked to the world's most powerful billionaires

A brand-new trilogy from USA TODAY *bestselling author Lynne Graham!*

The Blake heiresses have lived so long under the harsh rule of their father's iron fist, even the shackles of an arranged marriage seem like a reprieve—*at first!*

But they soon discover that they've jumped straight out of the frying pan…and into the fire. For their convenient husbands are men of the world—international, experienced and oh-so-devastatingly sexy!

Roccanti's Marriage Revenge

April—Zara's Story

Tricked!

Zara's very public engagement is hijacked by vengeful Italian billionaire Vitale Roccanti. The scandal they've created means there's no way left but down—*the aisle!*

A Deal at the Altar

May—Bee's story

Sold!

Bee is worth her weight in gold to Greek tycoon Sergios Demonides. But he needs her maternal skills rather than a trophy wife.

A Vow of Obligation

June—Tawny's story

Deceived!

Caught red-handed by her boss, Tawny is scandalized by Cazier's shocking proposal—a public engagement for her freedom!

Lynne Graham

A DEAL AT THE ALTAR

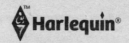

TORONTO NEW YORK LONDON
AMSTERDAM PARIS SYDNEY HAMBURG
STOCKHOLM ATHENS TOKYO MILAN MADRID
PRAGUE WARSAW BUDAPEST AUCKLAND

Recycling programs
for this product may
not exist in your area.

ISBN-13: 978-0-373-13067-2

A DEAL AT THE ALTAR

Copyright © 2012 by Lynne Graham

www.Harlequin.com

Printed in U.S.A.

All about the author...
Lynne Graham

Born of Irish/Scottish parentage, **LYNNE GRAHAM** has lived in Northern Ireland all her life. She has one brother. She grew up in a seaside village and now lives in a country house surrounded by a woodland garden, which is wonderfully private.

Lynne met her husband when she was fourteen; they married after she completed a degree at Edinburgh University. Lynne wrote her first book at fifteen—it was rejected everywhere. She started writing again when she was at home with her first child. It took several attempts before she was published, and she has never forgotten the delight of seeing that book for sale at the local newsagents.

Lynne always wanted a large family, and she now has five children. Her eldest, her only natural child, is in her twenties and is a university graduate. Her other children, who are every bit as dear to her heart, are adopted: two from Sri Lanka and two from Guatemala. In Lynne's home there is a rich and diverse cultural mix, which adds a whole extra dimension of interest and discovery to family life.

The family has two pets. Thomas, a very large and affectionate black cat, bosses the dog and hunts rabbits. The dog is Daisy, an adorable but not very bright West Highland white terrier, who loves being chased by the cat. At night, dog and cat sleep together in front of the kitchen stove.

Lynne loves gardening and cooking, collects everything from old toys to rock specimens and is crazy about every aspect of Christmas.

Other titles by Lynne Graham available in ebook:

Harlequin Presents®

CHAPTER ONE

'WHAT do I want to do about the Royale hotel group?' The speaker, a very tall and well-built Greek male with blue-black hair, raised an ebony brow and gave a sardonic laugh. 'Let's allow Blake to sweat for the moment...'

'Yes, sir.' Thomas Morrow, the British executive who had asked the question at the behest of his colleagues, was conscious of the nervous perspiration on his brow. One-on-one encounters with his powerhouse employer, one of the richest men in the world, were rare and he was keen not to say anything that might be deemed stupid or naive.

Everybody knew that Sergios Demonides did not suffer fools gladly. Unfortunately, priding himself on being a maverick, the Greek billionaire did not feel the need to explain the objectives behind his business decisions either, which could make life challenging for his executive team. Not so long ago the acquisition of the Royale hotel group at any price had seemed to be the goal and there was even a strong rumour that Sergios might be planning to marry the exquisite Zara Blake, the daughter of the man who owned the hotel chain. But after Zara had been pictured in the media in the arms of an Italian banker that rumour had died and Sergios's curious staff had not noticed their boss exhibiting the smallest sign of annoyance over the development.

'I took the original offer to Blake off the table. The price will come down now,' Sergios pointed out lazily, brilliant black eyes glittering at that prospect for more than anything else in life he liked to drive a hard bargain.

Purchasing the Royale group at an inflated price would have gone very much against the grain with him, but a couple of months ago Sergios had been prepared to do it and jump through virtually any hoop just to make that deal. *Why?* His beloved grandfather, Nectarios, who had started his legendary business empire at the helm of the very first Royale hotel in London, had been seriously ill at the time. But, mercifully, Nectarios was a tough old buzzard, Sergios thought fondly, and pioneering heart surgery in the USA had powered his recovery. Sergios now thought that the hotel chain would make a timely little surprise for his grandfather's eightieth birthday, but he no longer had any intention of paying over the odds for the gift.

As for the wife he had almost acquired as part of the deal, Sergios was relieved that fate had prevented him from making that mistake. Zara Blake, after all, had shown herself up as a beautiful little tart with neither honour nor decency. On the other hand her maternal instincts would have come in very useful where his children were concerned, he conceded grudgingly. Had it not been for the fact that his cousin's premature death had left Sergios responsible for his three young children, Sergios would not even have considered taking a second wife.

His handsome face hardened. One catastrophe in that department had been quite sufficient for Sergios. For the sake of those children, however, he had been prepared to bite the bullet and remarry. It would have been a marriage of convenience though, a public sham to gain a mother for the children and assuage his conscience. He knew nothing about kids and had never wanted any of his own but he knew his cousin's children were unhappy and that piqued his pride and his sense of honour.

'So, we're waiting for Blake to make the next move,' Thomas guessed, breaking the silence.

'And it won't be long. He's over-extended and under-funded with very few options left,' Sergios commented with growling satisfaction.

'You're a primary school teacher and good with young kids,' Monty Blake pointed out, seemingly impervious to his eldest daughter's expression of frank astonishment as she stood in his wood-panelled office. 'You'd make the perfect wife for Demonides—'

'No, stop right there!' Bee lifted a hand to physically emphasise that demand, her green eyes bright with disbelief as she used her other hand to push the heavy fall of chestnut-brown hair off her damp brow. Now she knew that her surprise and disquiet that her father should have asked her to come and see him were not unfounded. 'This is me, not Zara, you're talking to and I have no desire to marry an oversexed billionaire who needs some little woman at home to look after his kids—'

'Those kids are not his,' the older man broke in to remind her, as though that should make a difference to her. 'His cousin's death made him their guardian. By all accounts he didn't either want or welcome the responsibility—'

At that information, Bee's delicately rounded face only tightened with increased annoyance. She had plenty of experience with men who could not be bothered with children, not least with the man standing in front of her making sexist pronouncements. He might have persuaded her naive younger sister, Zara, to consider a marriage of convenience with the Greek shipping magnate, but Bee was far less impressionable and considerably more suspicious.

She had never sought her father's approval, which was just as well because as she was a mere daughter it had never been on offer to her. She was not afraid to admit that she didn't like or respect the older man, who had taken no interest in her as she grew up. He had also badly damaged her self-esteem at sixteen when he advised her that she needed to go on a diet and dye her hair a lighter colour. Monty Blake's image of female perfection was unashamedly blonde and skinny, while Bee was brunette and resolutely curvy. She focused on the desk photograph of her stepmother, Ingrid, a glamorous former Swedish model, blonde and thin as a rail.

'I'm sorry, I'm not interested, Dad,' Bee told him squarely, belatedly noticing that he wore an undeniable look of tiredness and strain. Perhaps he had come up with that outrageous suggestion that she marry Sergios Demonides because he was stressed out with business worries, she reasoned uncertainly.

'Well, you'd better get interested,' Monty Blake retorted sharply. 'Your mother and you lead a nice life. If the Royale hotel group crashes so that Demonides can pick it up for a song, the fallout won't only affect me and your stepmother but *all* my dependants...'

Bee tensed at that doom-laden forecast. 'What are you saying?'

'You know very well what I'm saying,' he countered impatiently. 'You're not as stupid as your sister—'

'Zara is *not*—'

'I'll come straight to the point. I've always been very generous to you and your mother...'

Uncomfortable with that subject though she was, Bee also liked to be fair. 'Yes, you have been,' she was willing to acknowledge.

It was not the moment to say that she had always thought his generosity towards her mother might be better described as 'conscience' money. Emilia, Bee's Spanish mother, had been Monty's first wife. In the wake of a serious car accident, Emilia had emerged from hospital as a paraplegic in a wheelchair. Bee had been four years old at the time and her mother had quickly realised that her young, ambitious husband was repulsed by her handicap. With quiet dignity, Emilia had accepted the inevitable and agreed to a separation. In gratitude for the fact that she had returned his freedom without a fuss, Monty had bought Emilia and her daughter a detached house in a modern estate, which he had then had specially adapted to her mother's needs. He had also always paid for the services of a carer to ensure that Bee was not burdened with round-the-clock responsibility for her mother. While the need to help out at home had necessarily restricted Bee's social life from a young age, she was painfully aware that only her father's financial support had made it possible for her to attend university, train as a teacher and actually take up the career that she loved.

'I'm afraid that unless you do what I'm asking you to do the gravy train of my benevolence stops here and now,' Monty Blake declared harshly. 'I own your mother's house. It's in my name and I can sell it any time I choose.'

Bee turned pale at that frank warning, shock winging through her because this was not a side of her father that she had ever come up against before. 'Why would you do something so dreadful to Mum?'

'Why should I care now?' Monty demanded curtly. 'I married your mother over twenty years ago and I've looked after her ever since. Most people would agree that I've more than paid my dues to a woman I was only married to for five years.'

'You know how much Mum and I appreciate everything that you have done for her,' Bee responded, her pride stung by the need to show that humility in the face of his obnoxious threatening behaviour.

'If you want my generosity to continue it will *cost* you,' the older man spelt out bluntly. 'I need Sergios Demonides to buy my hotels at the right price. And he was willing to do that until Zara blew him off and married that Italian instead—'

'Zara's deliriously happy with Vitale Roccanti,' Bee murmured tautly in her half-sister's defence. 'I don't see how I could possibly persuade a big tough businessman like Demonides to buy your hotels at a preferential price.'

'Well, let's face it, you don't have Zara's looks,' her father conceded witheringly. 'But as I understand it all Demonides wants is a mother for those kids he's been landed with and you'd make a damned sight better mother for them than Zara ever would have done—your sister can barely read! I bet he didn't know that when he agreed to marry her.'

Stiff with distaste at the cruelty of his comments about her sister, who suffered from dyslexia, Bee studied him coolly. 'I'm sure a man as rich and powerful as Sergios Demonides could find any number of women willing to marry him and play mummy to those kids. As you've correctly pointed out I'm not the ornamental type so I can't understand why you imagine he might be interested in me.'

Monty Blake released a scornful laugh. 'Because I know what he wants—Zara told me. He wants a woman who knows her place—'

'Well, then, he definitely doesn't want me,' Bee slotted in drily, her eyes flaring at that outdated expression that assumed female inferiority. 'And Zara's feistier than you seem to appreciate. I think he would have had problems with her too.'

'But you're the clever one who could give him exactly what he wants. You're much more practical than Zara ever was because you've never had it too easy—'

'Dad…?' Bee cut in, spreading her hands in a silencing motion. 'Why are we even having this insane conversation? I've only met Sergios Demonides once in my life and he barely looked at me.'

She swallowed back the unnecessary comment that the only part of her the Greek tycoon had noticed had appeared to be her chest.

'I want you to go to him and offer him a deal—the same deal he made with Zara. A marriage where he gets to do as he likes and buys my hotels at the agreed figure—'

'*Me*…go to *him* with a proposal of marriage?' Bee echoed in ringing disbelief. 'I've never heard anything so ridiculous in my life! The man would think I was a lunatic!'

Monty Blake surveyed her steadily. 'I believe you're clever enough to be convincing. If you can persuade him that you could be a perfect wife and mother for those little orphans you're that something extra that could put this deal back on the table for me. I need this sale and I need it now or everything I've worked for all my life is going to tumble down like a pack of cards. And with it will go your mother's security—'

'Don't threaten Mum like that.'

'But it's not an empty threat.' Monty shot his daughter an embittered look. 'The bank's threatening to pull the plug on my loans. My hotel chain is on the edge of disaster and right now that devil, Demonides, is playing a waiting game. I can't afford to wait. If I go down you and your mother will lose everything too,' he reminded her doggedly. 'Think about it and imagine it— no specially adapted house, day-to-day responsibility for Emilia, no life of your own any more…'

'Don't!' Bee exclaimed, disgusted by his coercive methods. 'I think you have to be off your head to think that Sergios Demonides would even consider marrying someone like me.'

'Perhaps I am but we're not going to know until you make the approach, are we?'

'You're crazy!' his daughter protested vehemently, aghast at what he was demanding of her.

Her father stabbed a finger in the air. 'I'll have a For Sale sign erected outside your mother's house this week if you don't at least go and see him.'

'I couldn't…I just *couldn't*!' Bee gasped, appalled by his persistence. 'Please don't do this to Mum.'

'I've made a reasonable request, Bee. I'm in a very tight corner. Why, after enjoying all my years of expensive support and education, shouldn't you try to help?'

'Oh, puh-lease,' Bee responded with helpless scorn at that smooth and inaccurate résumé of his behaviour as a parent. 'Demanding that I approach a Greek billionaire and ask him to marry me is a *reasonable* request? On what planet and in what culture would that be reasonable?'

'Tell him you'll take those kids off his hands and allow him to continue enjoying his freedom and I think you're in with a good chance,' the older man replied stubbornly.

'And what happens when I humiliate myself and he turns me down?'

'You'll have to pray that he says yes,' Monty Blake answered, refusing to give an inch in his desperation. 'After all, it is the *only* way that your mother's life is likely to continue as comfortably as it has done for years.'

'Newsflash, Dad. Life in a wheelchair is not comfortable,' his daughter flung at him bitterly.

'And life without my financial security blanket is likely to be even less comfortable,' he sliced back, determined to have the last word.

Minutes later, having failed to change her father's mind in any way, Bee left the hotel and caught the bus home to the house she still shared with her mother. She was cooking supper when her mother's care assistant, Beryl, brought Emilia back from a trip to the library. Wheeling into the kitchen, Emilia beamed at her daughter. 'I found a Catherine Cookson I haven't read!'

'I won't be able to get you off to sleep tonight now.' Looking down into her mother's worn face, aged and lined beyond her years by illness and suffering, Bee could have wept at the older woman's continuing determination to celebrate the smallest things in life. Emilia had lost so much in that accident but she never ever complained.

When she had settled her mother for the night, Bee sat down to mark homework books for her class of seven-year-olds. Her mind, however, refused to stay on the task. She could not stop thinking about what her father had told her. He had threatened her but he had also told her a truth that had ripped away her sense of security. After all, she had naively taken her father's continuing financial success for granted and assumed that he would always be in a position to ensure that her mother had no money worries.

Being Bee, she had to consider the worst-case scenario. If her mother lost her house and garden it would undoubtedly break her heart. The house had been modified for a disabled occupant so that Emilia could move easily within its walls. Zara had even designed raised flower beds for the back garden, which her mother could work at on good days. If the house was sold Bee had a salary and would naturally be able to rent an apartment *but* as she would not be able to afford a full-time carer for her mother any more she would have to give up work to look after her and would thus lose that salary. Monty Blake might cover the bills but there had never been a surplus or indeed a legal agreement that he provide financial support and Emilia had no savings. Without his assistance the two women would have to live on welfare benefits and all the little extras and outings that lightened and lifted her mother's difficult life would no longer be affordable. It was a gloomy outlook that appalled Bee, who had always been very protective of the older woman.

Indeed when she thought about Emilia losing even the little things that she cherished the prospect of proposing marriage to a very intimidating Greek tycoon became almost acceptable. So what if she made a fool of herself? Well, there was no 'if' about it, she would make a colossal fool of herself and he might well dine out on the story for years! He had seemed to her as exactly the sort of guy likely to enjoy other people's misfortunes.

Not that he hadn't enjoyed misfortunes of his own, Bee was willing to grudgingly concede. When her sister had planned to marry Sergios, Bee had researched him on the Internet and she had disliked most of what she had discovered. Sergios had only become a Demonides when he was a teenager with a string of petty crimes to his name. He had grown up fighting for survival in one of the roughest areas of Athens. At twenty-one he had married a beautiful Greek heiress and barely three years later he had buried her when she died carrying their unborn child. Yes, Sergios Demonides might be filthy rich and successful, but his personal life was generally a disaster zone.

Those facts aside, however, he also had a name for being an out-and-out seven-letter-word in business and with women. Popular report said that he was extremely intelligent and astute but that he was also famously arrogant, ruthless and cold, the sort of guy who, as a husband, would have given her sensitive sister Zara and her cute pet rabbit, Fluffy, nightmares. Fortunately Bee did not consider herself sensitive. Growing up without a father and forced to become an adult long before her time as she learned to cope with her mother's disability and dependence, Bee had forged a tougher shell.

At the age of twenty-four, Bee already knew that men were rarely attracted to that protective shell or the unadorned conservative wrapping that surrounded it. She wasn't pretty or feminine and the boys she had dated as she grew up had, with only one exception, been friends rather than lovers. She had never learned to flirt or play girlie games and thought that perhaps she was just too sensible. She had, however, for a blissful few months been deeply in love and desperately hurt when the relationship fell apart over the extent of her responsibility for her disabled mother. And while she couldn't have cared less about her appearance, she *was* clever and passing so many exams with distinction and continually winning prizes did, she had learned to her cost, scare off the opposite sex.

The men she met also tended to be put off when Bee spoke her mind even if it meant treading on toes. She hated injustice or cruelty in any form. She didn't do that fragile-little-woman thing her stepmother, Ingrid, was for ever flattering her father with. It was hardly surprising that even Zara, the sister she loved, had grown up with a healthy dose of that same fatal man-pleasing gene. Only her youngest sister, Tawny, born of her father's affair with his secretary, resembled Bee in that line. Bee had never known what it was to feel helpless until she found herself actually making an appointment to see Sergios Demonides…such a crazy idea, such a very pointless exercise.

Forty-eight hours after Bee won the tussle with her pride and made the appointment, Sergios's PA asked him if he was willing to see Monty Blake's daughter, Beatriz. Unexpectedly Sergios had instant recall of the brunette's furious grass-green eyes and magnificent breasts. A dinner in tiresome company had been rendered almost bearable by his enticing view of that gravity-defying bosom, although she had not appreciated the attention. But why the hell would Blake's elder daughter want to speak to him? Did she work with her father? Was she hoping to act as the older man's negotiator? He snapped his long brown fingers to bring an aide to his side and requested an immediate background report on Beatriz before granting her an appointment the next day.

The following afternoon, dressed in a grey trouser suit, which she usually reserved for interviews but which she was convinced gave her much-needed dignity, Bee waited in the reception area of the elegant stainless-steel and glass building that housed the London headquarters of SD Shipping. That Sergios had used his own initials to stamp his vast business empire with his powerful personality didn't surprise Bee at all. Her heart rate increased at the prospect that loomed ahead of her.

'Mr Demonides will see you now, Miss Blake,' the attractive receptionist informed her with a practised smile that Bee could not match.

Without warning Bee was feeling sick with nerves. She was too intelligent not to contemplate the embarrassment awaiting her without inwardly cringing. She was quick to remind herself that the Greek billionaire was just a big hulking brute with too much money and an inability to ignore a low neck on a woman's dress. She reddened, recalling the evening gown with the plunge neckline that she had borrowed from a friend for that stupid meal. While his appraisal had made Bee blush like a furnace and had reminded her why she usually covered up those particular attributes, she had been stunned by his apparent indifference to her beautiful sister, Zara.

When Beatriz Blake came through the door of Sergios's office with a firm step in her sensible shoes, he instantly recognised that he was not about to be treated to any form of charm offensive. Her boxy colourless trouser suit did nothing for her womanly curves. Her rich brown hair was dragged back from her face and she wore not a scrap of make-up. To a man accustomed to highly groomed women her lackadaisical attitude towards making a good impression struck him as almost rude.

'I'm a very busy man, Beatriz. I don't know what you're doing here but I expect you to keep it brief,' he told her impatiently.

For a split second Sergios Demonides towered over Bee like a giant building casting a long tall shadow and she took a harried step back, feeling crowded by his sheer size and proximity. She had forgotten how big and commanding he was, from his great height to his broad shoulders and long powerful legs. He was also, much though it irritated her to admit it, a staggeringly handsome man with luxuriant blue-black hair and sculpted sun-darkened features. The sleek unmistakeable assurance of great wealth oozed from the discreet gleam of his thin gold watch and cufflinks to the spotless white of his shirt and the classy tailoring of his dark business suit.

She collided with eyes the colour of burnished bronze that had the impact of a sledgehammer and cut off her breathing at its source. It was as if nerves were squeezing her throat tight and her heart started hammering again.

'My father asked me to see you on his behalf,' she began, annoyed by the breathlessness making her voice sound low and weak.

'You're a primary school teacher. What could you possibly have to say that I would want to hear?' Sergios asked with brutal frankness.

'I think you'll be surprised…' Bee compressed her lips, her voice gathering strength as reluctant amusement briefly struck her. 'Well, I *know* you'll be surprised.'

Surprises were rare and even less welcome in Sergios's life. He was a control freak and knew it and had not the smallest urge to change.

'A little while back you were planning to marry my sister, Zara.'

'It wouldn't have worked,' Sergios responded flatly.

Bee breathed in deep and slow while her white-knuckled hands gripped the handles of her bag. 'Zara told me exactly what you wanted out of marriage.'

While wondering where the strange dialogue could possibly be leading, Sergios tried not to grit his teeth visibly. 'That was most indiscreet of her.'

Discomfiture sent colour flaming into Bee's cheeks, accentuating the deep green of her eyes. 'I'm just going to put my cards on the table and get to the point.'

Sergios rested back against the edge of his polished contemporary desk and surveyed her in a manner that was uniquely discouraging, 'I'm waiting,' he said when she hesitated.

His impatient silence hummed like bubbling water ready to boil over.

Beneath her jacket, Bee breathed in so deep her bosom swelled and almost popped the buttons on her fitted blouse and for a split second Sergios dropped his narrowed gaze there as the fabric pulled taut over that full swell, whose bounty he still vividly recalled.

'My father utilised a certain amount of pressure to persuade me to come and see you,' she admitted uncomfortably. 'I told him it was crazy but here I am.'

'Yes, here…you…are,' Sergios framed in a tone of yawning boredom. 'Still struggling to come to the point.'

'Dad wanted me to offer myself in Zara's place.' Bee squeezed out that admission and watched raw incredulity laced with astonished hauteur flare in his face while hot pink embarrassment surged into hers. 'I know, I told you it was crazy but he wants that hotel deal and he thinks that a suitable wife added into the mix could make a difference.'

'Suitable? You're certainly not in the usual run of women who aspire to marry me.' Sergios delivered that opinion bluntly.

And it was true. Beatriz Blake was downright plain in comparison to the gorgeous women who pursued him wherever he went, desperate to attract his attention and get their greedy hands on, if not the ultimate prize of a wedding ring, some token of his wealth. But somewhere deep in his mind at that instant a memory was stirring.

'Homely women make the best wives,' his grandfather had once contended. 'Your grandmother was unselfish, loyal and caring. I couldn't have asked for a better wife. My home was kept like a palace, my children were loved, and my word was law. She never gave me a second of concern. Think well before you marry a beauty, who demands more and gives a lot less.'

Having paled at that unnecessary reminder of her limitations, Bee made a fast recovery and lifted her chin. 'Obviously I'm not blonde and beautiful but I'm convinced that I would be a more appropriate choice than Zara ever was for the position.'

A kind of involuntary fascination at the level of her nerve was holding Sergios taut. His straight black brows drew together in a frown. 'You speak as though the role of being my wife would be a job.'

'Isn't it?' Bee came back at him boldly with that challenge. 'From what I understand you only want to marry to have a mother for your late cousin's children and I could devote myself to their care full-time, something Zara would never have been willing to do. I also—'

'Be silent for a moment,' Sergios interrupted, studying her with frowning attention. 'What kind of pressure did your father put on you to get you to come here and spout this nonsense?'

Bee went rigid before she tossed her head back in sudden defiance, wondering why she should keep her father's coercion a secret. Her pride demanded that she be honest. 'I have a severely disabled mother and if the sale of the Royale hotel chain falls through my father has threatened to sell our home and stop paying for Mum's care assistant. I'm not dependent on him but Mum is and I don't want to see her suffer. Her life is challenging enough.'

'I'm sure it is.' Sergios was unwillingly impressed by her motivation. Evidently Monty Blake was crueller within his family circle than Sergios would ever have guessed. Even Nectarios, his grandfather and one of the most ruthless men Sergios had ever met, would have drawn the line at menacing a disabled ex-wife. As for Beatriz, he could respect her honesty and her family loyalty, traits that said a lot about the kind of woman she was. She wasn't here for his enviable lifestyle or his money, she was here because she didn't have a choice. That was not a flattering truth but Sergios loathed flattery, having long since recognised that few people saw past his immense wealth and power to the man behind it all.

'So, tell me why you believe that you would make a better wife than your sister?' Sergios urged, determined to satisfy his curiosity and intrigued by her attitude towards marriage. A wife as an employee? It was a new take on the traditional role that appealed to him. A businessman to the core, he was quick to see the advantages of such an arrangement. A paid wife would be more likely to respect his boundaries while still making the effort to please him, he reasoned thoughtfully. There could be little room for messy human emotion and misunderstanding in such a practical agreement.

'I would be less demanding. I'm self-sufficient, sensible. I probably wouldn't cost you very much either as I'm not very interested in my appearance,' Bee pointed out, her full pink mouth folding as if vanity could be considered a vice. 'I'm also very good with kids.'

'What would you do with a six-year-old boy painting pictures on the walls?'

Bee frowned. 'Talk to him.'

'But he doesn't talk back. His little brother keeps on trying to cling to me and the toddler just stares into space,' Sergios told her in a driven undertone, his concern and incomprehension of such behaviour patent. 'Why am I telling you that?'

Surprised by his candour, Bee reckoned it was a sign that the children's problems were very much on his mind 'You thought I might have an answer for you?'

With a warning knock the door opened and someone addressed him in what she assumed to be Greek. He gave a brief answer and returned his attention to Bee. Something about that assessing look made her stiffen. 'I'll think over your proposition,' he drawled softly, startling her. 'But be warned, I'm not easy to please.'

'I knew that the first time I looked at you,' Bee countered, taking in the sardonic glitter of his eyes, the hard, uncompromising bone structure and that stubborn sensual mouth. It was very much the face of a tough guy, resistant to any counsel but his own.

'Next you'll be telling me you can read my fortune from my palm,' Sergios retorted with mocking cool.

Bee walked out of his office in a daze. He had said he would consider her proposition. Had that only been a polite lie? Somehow she didn't think he would have given her empty words. But if he was seriously considering her as a wife, where did that leave her? Fathoms deep in shock? For since Bee had automatically assumed that Sergios Demonides would turn her down she had not, at any stage, actually considered the possibility of becoming his wife...

CHAPTER TWO

FOUR days later, Bee emerged from the gates of the primary school where she worked and noticed a big black limousine parked just round the corner.

'Miss Blake?' A man in a suit with the build of a bouncer approached her. 'Mr Demonides would like to offer you a lift home.'

Bee blinked and stared at the long glossy limo with its tinted windows. How had he found out where she worked? While wondering what on earth Sergios Demonides was playing at, she saw no option other than to accept. Why queue for a bus when a limo was on offer? she reflected ruefully. Had he come in person to deliver his negative answer? Why would he take the trouble to do that? A man of his exalted status rarely put himself out for others. As a crowd of colleagues and parents parted to give Bee and her bulky companion a clear passage to the opulent vehicle self-conscious pink warmed her cheeks because people were staring.

'Beatriz,' Sergios acknowledged with a grave nod, glancing up from his laptop.

As Bee slid into the luxury vehicle she was disturbingly conscious of the sheer animal charisma that he exuded from every pore. He was all male in the most primal sense of the word. Smell the testosterone, one of her university friends would have quipped. The faint tang of some expensive masculine cologne flared her nostrils, increasing her awareness. She felt her nipples pinch tight beneath her bra and she went rigid, deeply disconcerted by her pronounced awareness of the sexual charge he put out. Her shielded gaze fell on his lean masculine profile, noting the dark shadow of stubble outlining his angular jaw. He was badly in need of a shave. It was the only sign in his otherwise immaculate appearance that he was nearing the end of his working day rather than embarking on its beginning. Aware that her hair was tossed by the breeze and her raincoat, skirt and knee-high boots were more comfortable than smart, she was stiff and awkward and questioning why because as a rule her sole concern about her appearance was that she be clean and tidy.

As the limousine pulled away from the pavement Sergios flipped shut his laptop and turned his arrogant head to look at her. His frown was immediate. She was a mess in her unfashionable, slightly shabby clothing. Yet she had flawless skin, lovely eyes and thick glossy hair, advantages that most women would have made the effort to enhance. For the first time he wondered why she didn't bother.

'To what do I owe the honour?' Bee enquired, watching him push the laptop away. He had beautiful shapely hands, she registered, and then tensed at that surprising thought.

'I'm leaving for New York this evening and I would like you to meet my children before I go.'

'Why?' Green eyes suddenly wide with confusion, Bee stared back at him. 'Why do you want me to meet them?'

A very faint smile curled the corners of his wide sensual mouth. 'Obviously because I'm considering you for the job.'

'But you *can't* be!' Bee told him in disbelief.

'I am. Your father played a winning hand sending you to see me,' Sergios fielded, amused by her astonishment, which was laced with a dismay that almost made him laugh out loud. She was a refreshing woman.

Her well-defined brows pleated and she frowned. 'I just don't understand…you could marry anybody!'

'Don't underestimate yourself,' Sergios responded, his thoughts on the enquiries and references he had gathered on her behalf since their last meeting. He had vetted her a good deal more thoroughly than he had vetted her flighty sister, Zara. 'According to my sources you're a loyal, devoted daughter and a gifted and committed teacher. I believe that you could offer those children exactly what they need—'

'Where did you get that information from?' Bee asked angrily.

'There are private investigation firms which can offer such details within hours for the right price,' Sergios fielded with colossal calm. 'Naturally I checked you out and I was impressed with what I learned about you.'

But I wasn't *seriously* offering to marry you, she almost snapped back at him before she thought better of that revealing admission and hastily swallowed it back. After all her father's threat still hung over her and his financial security was integral to her mother's support system. Take away that security and life as her mother knew it would be at an end. Suddenly Bee was looking down a long, dark, intimidating tunnel at a future she could no longer predict and accepting that if Sergios Demonides decided that he did want to marry her, she would be in no position to refuse him.

'If your cousin's children are disturbed, I have no experience with that sort of problem,' Bee warned him quietly. 'I have no experience of raising children either and I'm not a miracle worker.'

'I don't believe in miracles, so I'm not expecting one,' Sergios said very drily, resting sardonic golden eyes on her strained face. 'There would also be conditions which you would have to fulfil to meet my requirements.'

Bee said nothing. Still reeling in shock at the concept of marrying him, she did not trust herself to speak. As for his expectations, she was convinced they would be high and that he would have a very long list of them. Unhappily for her, Sergios Demonides was unaccustomed to settling for anything less than perfection and the very best in any field. She dug out her phone and rang her mother to warn her that she would be late home. By the time she finished the call the limousine was already filtering down a driveway adorned with silver birch trees just coming into leaf. They drew up outside a detached house large and grand enough to be described as a mansion.

'My London base.' Sergios shot her a rapier-eyed

glance from level dark eyes. 'One of your duties as my wife would be taking charge of my various homes and ensuring that the households run smoothly.'

The word 'wife', allied to that other word, 'duties', sounded horribly nineteenth century to Bee's ears. 'Are you a domestic tyrant?' she enquired.

Sergios sent her a frowning appraisal. 'Is that a joke?'

'No, but there is something very Victorian about mentioning the word wife in the same sentence as duties.'

His handsome mouth quirked. 'You first referred to the role as a job and I prefer to regard it in the same light.'

But Bee very much liked the job she already had and registered in some consternation that she was literally being asked to put her money where her mouth was. She had done what her father had asked her to do without thinking through the likely consequences of success. Now those consequences had well and truly come home to roost with her. As she accompanied Sergios into a sizeable foyer, he issued instructions to the manservant greeting him and escorted Bee into a massive drawing room.

'Unlike your sister, you're very quiet,' he remarked.

'You've taken me by surprise,' Bee admitted ruefully.

'You look bewildered. Why?' Sergios breathed, his bronzed eyes impatient. 'I have no desire for the usual kind of wife. I don't want the emotional ties, the demands or the restrictions, but on a practical basis a woman to fulfil that role would be a very useful addition to my life.'

'Perhaps I just don't see what's in it for me—apart from you buying my father's hotels which would hopefully ensure my mother's security for the foreseeable future,' Bee volunteered frankly.

'If I married you, *I* would ensure your mother's security for the rest of her life,' Sergios extended with quiet carrying emphasis, his dark deep drawl vibrating in the big room. 'Even if we were to part at a later date you would never have to worry about her care again, nor would she have to look to your father for support. I will personally ensure that your mother has everything she requires, including the very best of medical treatment available to someone with her condition.'

His words engulfed her like a crashing burst of thunder heralding a brighter dawn. Instantly Bee thought of the expensive extras that could improve Emilia Blake's quality of life. In place of Bee's home-made efforts, regular professional physiotherapy sessions might be able to strengthen Emilia's wasted limbs and something might be found to ease the breathing difficulties that sometimes afflicted her. Sergios, Bee appreciated suddenly, was rich enough to make a huge difference to her mother's life.

A young woman in a nanny uniform entered the room with a baby about eighteen months old in her arms and two small children trailing unenthusiastically in their wake.

'Thank you. Leave the children with us,' Sergios instructed.

Set down on the carpet the youngest child instantly began to howl, tears streaming down her little screwed-up face, a toddler of about three years old grabbed hold of Sergios's trousered leg while the older boy came to a suspicious halt several feet away.

'It's all right, pet.' Bee scooped up the baby and the little girl stopped mid-howl, settling anxious blue eyes on her. 'What's her name?'

'Eleni…and this is Milo,' Sergios told her, detaching the clinging toddler from his leg with difficulty and giving him a little helpful prod in Bee's direction as if he was hoping that the child would embrace her instead.

'And you have to be Paris,' Bee said to the older boy as she crouched down to greet Milo. 'My sister Zara told me that you got a new bike for your birthday.'

Paris didn't smile but he moved closer as Bee sank down on the sofa with the baby girl in her arms. Milo, clearly desperate for attention, clambered up beside her and tried to get on her lap with his sister but there wasn't enough room. 'Hello, Milo.'

'Paris, remember your manners,' Sergios interposed sternly.

With a scared look, Paris extended a skinny arm to shake hands formally, his eyes slewing evasively away from hers. Bee invited him to sit down beside her and told him that she was a teacher. When she asked him about the school he attended he shot her a frightened look and hurriedly glanced away. It did not take a genius to guess that Paris could be having problems at school. Of the three children, Milo was the most normal, a bundle of toddler energy in need of attention and entertainment. Paris, however, was tense and troubled while the little girl was very quiet and worryingly unresponsive.

After half an hour Sergios had seen enough to convince him that Beatriz Blake was the woman he needed to smooth out the rough and troublesome places in his life. Her warmth and energy drew the children and she was completely relaxed with them where her sister had been nervous and, while friendly, over-anxious to please. Bee, on the other hand, emanated a calm authority that ensured respect. He called the nanny back to remove the children again.

'You mentioned conditions…' Bee reminded him, returning to their earlier conversation and striving to stick to necessary facts. Yet when she tried to accept that she was actually considering marrying the Greek billionaire the idea seemed so remote and unreal and impossible that her thoughts swam in a sea of bemusement.

'Yes.' Poised by the window with fading light gleaming over his luxuriant black hair and accenting the hard angles and hollows of his handsome features, Sergios commanded her full attention without even trying. His next words, however, took her very much by surprise.

'I have a mistress. Melita is not negotiable,' Sergios informed her coolly. 'Occasionally I have other interests as well. I am discreet. I do not envisage any headlines about that aspect of my life.'

The level of such candour when she had become accustomed to his cool reserve left Bee reeling in shock. He had a mistress called Melita? Was that a Greek name? Whatever, he was not faithful to his mistress and clearly not a one-woman man. Bee could feel her cheeks inflame as her imagination filled with the kind of colourful images she did not want to have in his vicinity. She lowered her lashes in embarrassment, her rebellious brain still engaged in serving up a creative picture of that lean bronzed body of his entangled with that of a sinuous sexy blonde.

'I do not expect intimacy with you,' Sergios spelt out. 'On the other hand if you decide that you want a child of your own it would be selfish of me to deny you that option—'

'Well, then, there's always IVF,' Bee broke in hurriedly.

'From what I've heard it's not that reliable.'

Bee was now studying her feet with fixed attention. He had a mistress. He didn't expect to share a bed with her. But where did that leave her? A wife who wasn't a wife except in name.

'What sort of a life am I supposed to lead?' Bee asked him abruptly, looking up, green eyes glinting like fresh leaves in rain.

'Meaning?' Sergios prompted, pleased that she had demonstrated neither annoyance nor interest on the subject of his mistress. But then why should she care what he did? That was exactly the attitude he wanted her to take.

'Are you expecting me to take lovers as well… discreetly?' Bee queried, studying him while her colour rose and burned like scalding hot irons on her cheeks and she fought her embarrassment with all her might. It was a fair question, a sensible question and she refused to let prudishness prevent her from asking it.

His dark eyes glittered gold with anger. 'Of course not.'

Bee was frowning. 'I'm trying to understand how you expect such a marriage to work. You surely can't be suggesting that a woman of my age should accept a future in which any form of physical intimacy is against the rules?' she quantified very stiffly, fighting her mortification every step of the way.

Put like that her objection sounded reasonable but Sergios could no more have accepted the prospect of an unfaithful wife than he could have cut off his right arm. Features taut and grim, his big powerful length rigid, he breathed with the clarity of strong feeling, 'I could not agree to you taking lovers.'

'That old hypocritical double standard,' Bee murmured, strangely amused by his appalled reaction and not even grasping why she should feel that way. So what was good for the goose was not, in this case, good for the gander? Yet she could barely believe that she was even having such a discussion with him. After all, she was a twenty-four-year-old virgin, a piece of information that would no doubt shock him almost as much as the idea of a wife with an independent sexual appetite.

In response to that scornful comment, Sergios shot her a seething appraisal, his dark eyes flaming like hot coals. 'Don't speak to me in that tone…'

Lesson one, Bee noted, he has a very volatile temper. She breathed in deep, quelling her wicked stab of amusement at his incredulous reaction to the idea of an adulterous wife. 'I asked you a reasonable question and you did not give me a reasonable answer. How long do you expect this marriage to last?'

'At least until the children grow up.'

'My youth,' Bee remarked without any emotion, but it was true. By the time the children acquired independence her years of youth would be long gone.

Sergios was studying her, recalling those lush violin curves in the evening gown she had worn at their first meeting. Full pouting breasts, generous womanly hips. He was startled when that mental picture provoked the heavy tightness of arousal at his groin.

'Then we make it a real marriage,' Sergios fielded with sardonic bite, blanking out his physical response with male impatience. 'That is the only other possible option on the table. If you want a man in your bed you will have me, no other.'

The flush in Bee's cheeks swept up to her brow and her dismayed eyes skimmed away from the intrusion of his. 'I don't really wish to continue this discussion but I should say that while you have other women in your life I would not be willing to enter an intimate relationship with you.'

'We're wasting time with this nonsense and we're adults. We will deal with such problems as and when they arise,' Sergios delivered curtly. 'There will be a pre-nuptial contract for you to sign—'

'You mentioned your homes and your, er…mistress. What other conditions are you planning to impose?'

'Nothing that I think need concern you. Our lawyers can deal with the contracts. If you choose to argue about

terms you may do so through them,' Sergios completed
in a crushing tone of finality. 'Now, if you will excuse
me, I will have you driven home. I have business to take
care of before I leave for New York.'

Bee, who had had a vague idea that he might invite
her to stay to dinner, learned her mistake. She smoothed
down her raincoat and rose slowly upright. 'I have a
condition as well. You would have to agree to be polite,
respectful and considerate of my happiness at all times.'

As that unanticipated demand hit him Sergios froze
halfway to the door, wondering if she was criticising
his manners. Since he had reached eighteen years of
age before appreciating that certain courtesies even existed, he was unusually sensitive to the suggestion. He
turned back, brooding black eyes glittering below the
lush fan of his lashes. 'That would be a tall order. I'm
selfish, quick-tempered and often curt. I expect my staff
to adapt to my ways.'

'If I marry you I won't be a member of your staff.
I'll be somewhere between a wife and an employee.
You will have to make allowances and changes.' Bee
studied him expectantly, for it would be disastrous if
she allowed him to assume that he could have everything his way. She had no illusions about the fact that
she was dealing with a very powerful personality, who
would ride roughshod over her needs and wishes and
ignore them altogether if it suited him to do so.

Sergios was taken aback at her nerve in challenging
him, viewing him with those cool assessing green eyes
as though he were an intellectual puzzle to be solved.
His stubborn jaw line squared. 'I may make some al-

lowances but I will call the shots. If we're going ahead with this arrangement, I want the wedding to take place soon so that you can move in here to be with the children.'

Consternation filled Bee's face. 'But I can't leave my mother—'

'You're a teacher, good at talking but not at listening,' Sergios chided with a curled lip. '*Listen* to what I tell you. Your mother will be taken care of in every possible way.'

'In every possible way that facilitates what *you* want!' Bee slammed back at him with angry emphasis.

He raised a brow, sardonic amusement in his intent dark gaze. 'Would you really expect anything different from me?'

CHAPTER THREE

LIFE as Bee knew it began to change very soon after that thought-provoking parting from Sergios.

Indeed Bee came home from school the very next day to find her mother troubled by the fact that her father had made an angry phone call to her that same afternoon.

'Monty told me that you're getting married,' Emilia Blake recounted with a look of frank disbelief. 'But I told him that you weren't even seeing anyone.'

Bee went pink. 'I didn't tell you but—'

Her mother stared at her with wide, startled eyes. 'My goodness, there is someone! But you only go out twice a week to your exercise classes—'

Bee grimaced and reached for her mother's frail hands. Not for anything would she have told the older woman any truth that might upset her. Indeed when it came to her mother's peace of mind, Bee was more than ready to lie. 'I'm sorry I wasn't more honest with you. I do want you to be happy for me.'

'So, obviously you weren't at classes all those evenings,' Emilia assumed in some amusement while she studied her blushing daughter with fond pride in her shadowed eyes. 'I'm so pleased. Your father and I haven't set you a very good example and I know you haven't had the same choices as other girls your age—'

'You still haven't told me what my father was angry about,' Bee cut in anxiously.

'Some business deal he's involved in with your future husband hasn't gone the way he hoped,' Emilia responded in a dismissive tone. 'What on earth does he expect you to do about it? Take my advice, don't get involved.'

Dismayed by her explanation, Bee had tensed. 'Exactly what did Dad say?'

'You know how moody he can be when things don't go his way. Tell me about Sergios—isn't he the man you met at that dinner your father invited you to a couple of months ago?'

'Yes.' So, although the marriage was going ahead, it seemed that her father was not to profit as richly as he had expected from the deal. Clearly that was why the older man was angry, but Bee thought there was a rare justice to the news that her sacrifice was unlikely to enrich her father: threats did not deserve a reward.

'My word, you've been having a genuine whirlwind romance,' Emilia gathered with a blossoming smile of approval. 'Are you sure that this Sergios is the man for you, Bee?'

Bee recalled Sergios Demonides's assurance that she would never again have to look to her father to support her mother. She remembered the fearless impact of those shrewd dark eyes and although she was apprehensive about the future she had signed up for she did believe that Sergios would stand by his word. 'Yes, Mum. Yes, I'm sure.'

Sergios phoned that evening to tell her that a member of his personal staff would be liaising with her over the wedding arrangements. He suggested that she hand in her notice immediately. His impatience came as a surprise when he had seemingly been content to wait several months before taking her sister Zara to the altar. He then followed that bombshell up with the news that he expected her to move to Greece after the wedding.

'But you have a house here,' Bee protested.

'I will visit London regularly but Greece is my home.'

'When you were planning to marry Zara—'

'Stop there—you and I will reach our own arrangements,' Sergios cut in deflatingly.

'I don't want to leave my mother alone in London.'

'Your mother will accompany us to Greece—but only after we have enjoyed a suitable newly married period of togetherness. I have already issued instructions to have appropriate accommodation organised for her. Have you heard from your father yet?'

In shock at the news that he was already making plans for her mother to accompany them to Greece, Bee was in a complete daze, her every expectation blown apart. On every issue he seemed to be one step ahead of her. 'I believe he was annoyed about something when he was talking to my mother today,' she admitted reluctantly.

'Your father did not get the deal he wanted,' Sergios

informed her bluntly. 'But that is nothing to do with you and so I told him on your behalf.'

'Did you indeed?' Bee questioned with a frown, her hackles rising at the increasingly authoritarian note in his explanations. Acting as chief spokesperson for the women in his life evidently came very naturally to Sergios. If she wasn't careful to keep his controlling streak within bounds, Bee thought darkly, he would soon have her behaving with all the self-will of a glove puppet.

'You are the woman I'm going to marry. It is not appropriate for your father to speak of either you or your mother with disrespect and I have warned him in that regard.'

Bee's blood ran cold in her veins, for she could picture the scene and the warning with Monty Blake raging recklessly and Sergios cold as ice and equally precise in his razor-sharp cutting edge. Her father was outspoken in temper but Sergios was altogether a more guarded and astute individual.

'How soon can you move into my London house?' Sergios pressed. 'It would please me if you could make that move this week.'

'*This* week?' Bee exclaimed in dismay.

'The wedding will be soon. I'm out of the country and the domestic staff are in charge of the children right now. If possible I would prefer you to be in the house while I'm away. If you're concerned about your mother being alone, you need not be—I've already requested a live-in companion for her from a vetted source.'

Bee came off the phone feeling unusually harassed

as she accepted that regardless of how she felt about it, her life was about to be turned upside down. Although she could not fault Sergios for his wish that she become involved with the children as soon as possible, she felt very much like an employee having her extensive duties listed and held over her head. As she had already told her mother about the three orphaned kids in Sergios's life, Emilia Blake was quick to understand her daughter's position.

'You really *must* put Sergios and those children first, Bee,' the older woman instructed worriedly. 'You mustn't make me more of a burden than I already am. I'll manage, I always have.'

Bee gently squeezed her parent's shoulder. 'You've never been a burden to me.'

'Sergios expects to come first and that's normal for a man who wants to marry you,' Emilia told her daughter. 'Don't let me become a bone of contention between you.'

Having drawn up innumerable lists and tendered her letter of resignation, for it was the last day of the spring term, Bee attended her evening pole exercise class and worked up a sweat while she tried not to fret about the many things that she still had to do. The list grew even longer after a visit from Annabel, the glossily efficient PA Sergios had put in charge of the wedding.

'I'm to have a consultation with a personal stylist and shopper?' Bee repeated weakly, staring down at the heavy schedule of appointments already set up for her over the Easter break that began that weekend. As well as a consultation with an upmarket legal firm concerning the pre-nuptial agreement, there was a day-long booking at a famous beauty salon. 'That's ridiculous. That's got nothing to do with the wedding.'

'Mr Demonides gave me my instructions,' Annabel told her in a steely tone.

Bee swallowed hard and compressed her lips. She would argue her case directly with Sergios. Possibly he thought a makeover was every woman's dream but Bee felt deeply insulted by the proposition. Her mother's new live-in companion/carer arrived that same evening and Bee chatted to her and helped her to settle in before she packed her own case ready for her move into Sergios's house the next morning.

When she arrived there she was shown upstairs into a palatial bedroom suite furnished with every possible necessity and luxury, right down to headed notepaper on a dainty feminine desk. The household seemed to operate just like an exclusive hotel. A maid came to the door to offer to unpack for her. Overcoming her discomfort at the prospect of being waited on by the staff, Bee smiled in determined agreement and went off to find the children instead.

Only Eleni, the youngest, however, was at home. Paris was at school and Milo was at a play group, the nanny explained. A rota of three nannies looked after the children round the clock. Bee found out what she needed to know about the children's basic routine and got down on her knees on the nursery carpet to play with Eleni. Initially when she was close by and utilised eye contact the little girl was more responsive but her attention was hard to hold. When the wind caught the door and it slammed shut Bee flinched from the loud noise but noted in surprise that Eleni did not react at all.

'Has her hearing been checked?' Bee asked with a frown.

The newly qualified nanny, who had replaced someone else and only recently, had no idea. During the preceding months the children had suffered several changes in that line and had enjoyed little continuity of care. Having tracked down the children's health record booklets and drawn another blank, Bee finally phoned the medical practice to enquire. She discovered that Eleni had missed out on a standard hearing check-up a couple of months earlier and she made a fresh appointment for the child. When she returned to the nursery the nanny was engaged in conducting her own basic tests and even to the untrained eye it did seem as though the little girl might have a problem with her hearing.

Milo, who was indiscriminately affectionate with almost everybody, greeted her as though they were long-lost friends. She was reading a picture book to the little boy as he dropped off for a nap when Paris appeared in the nursery doorway and frowned at the sight of her with his little brother.

'Are you looking after us now?' Paris asked thinly.

'For some of the time. You won't need so many nannies because I'll be living here from now on. Sergios and I will be getting married in a few weeks.' Bee explained, striving to sound much calmer than she actually felt about that event.

Paris shot her a resentful glance and walked past

into his own room, carefully shutting the door behind him to underline his desire for privacy. Resolving to respect his wishes until she had visited his school and met his teacher, Bee suppressed a rueful sigh. She was a stranger. What more could she expect? Establishing a relationship with children who had lost their parents, their home and everything familiar only months before would take time and a good deal of trust on their part and she had to hope that Sergios was prepared for the reality that only time would improve the situation.

Forty-eight hours later, it was a novelty for Sergios to return to a house with a woman in residence and not worry about what awaited him. He could still vividly remember when he had never known what might be in store for him when he entered his own home. That experience had left him with an unshakable need to conserve his own space. Bee didn't count, he told himself irritably, she was here for the kids, not for him personally and she would soon learn to respect his privacy. He was taken aback, however, when his housekeeper informed him that Bee had gone out. He was even less impressed when he rang her cell phone and she admitted that she was travelling back on public transport.

'I wasn't expecting you back this soon...I was visiting my mother,' she told him defensively.

When Bee finally walked back into the mansion, she was flushed and breathless from walking very fast from the bus stop and thoroughly resentful of the censorious tone Sergios had used with her on the phone. Didn't he think she had a right to go out? Was she supposed to ask for permission first? Was her life to be entirely consumed by his? Heavy dark brown hair flopping untidily round her face, she stepped into the echoing hall.

Sergios appeared in a doorway and she lost her breath at that first glimpse, his impact thrumming through her like a sudden collision with a brick wall. He was still dressed in a black business suit and striped shirt, his only hint of informality the loosening of his tie. He looked like an angry dark angel, lean strong features taut, stubborn jaw line squared and once again he needed a shave. Stubble suited him though, sending his raw masculine sex appeal right off the charts, she conceded numbly, reeling in shock from the sudden loud thump of her heartbeat in her ears and the dryness of her mouth.

Sergios subjected his flustered bride-to-be to a hard scrutiny. From her chaotic hair to her ill-fitting jeans she was a mess. He realised that he was eager for the makeover to commence. 'I gave orders that if you went out you were to use a car and driver,' he reminded her flatly.

Bee reacted with a pained look. 'A bit much for a girl used to travelling by bus and tube.'

'But you are no longer that girl. You are the woman who is to become my wife,' Sergios retorted crisply. 'And I expect you to adapt accordingly. I am a wealthy man and you could be targeted by a mugger or even a kidnapper. Personal security must now become an integral part of your lifestyle.'

The reference to kidnapping cooled the heated words on Bee's ready tongue and, although she had stiffened, she nodded her head. 'I'll remember that in future.'

Satisfied, Sergios spread wide the door behind him. 'I want to talk to you.'

'Yes, we do need to talk,' Bee allowed, although in truth she wanted to run upstairs to her bedroom and stay there until her adolescent hormonal reaction to him died a natural death and stopped embarrassing her. Her face felt hot as a fire. It had been such a long time since a man had had that effect on her. When it had happened in his office she had assumed it was simply the effect of nerves and mortification but this time around she was less naive and ready to be honest with herself. As a physical specimen, Sergios Demonides was without parallel. He was absolutely gorgeous and few women would be impervious to his powerful attraction. That was all it was, she told herself urgently as she walked past him, her head held high, into a room furnished like an upmarket office. He had buckets of lethal sex appeal and all her body was telling her was that she had a healthy set of hormones. It was that simple, that basic, nothing to fret about. It certainly did not mean that she was genuinely attracted to him.

Sergios asked Bee about the children and she relaxed a little, telling him that Eleni had performed very poorly at her hearing test and the doctor suspected that she was suffering from glue ear. The toddler was to be examined by a consultant with a view to receiving treatment. Bee went on to talk about the picture that Paris had drawn on his bedroom wall. She considered his depiction of his once-happy family complete with parents and home to be self-explanatory. He had no photos of his late parents and Bee asked Sergios if there was a reason for that.

'I thought it would be less upsetting that way—he has to move on.'

'I think Paris needs the time to grieve and that family photos would help,' Bee pronounced with care.

'I put his parents' personal effects into storage. I'll have them checked for photo albums,' Sergios proffered, surprising her by accepting her opinion.

'I think that all that is wrong is that the children have endured too many changes in a short space of time. They need a settled home life.'

Sergios expelled his breath with a slight hiss, his expression grim. 'I've done my best but clearly it wasn't good enough. I know nothing about children. I don't even know how to talk to them.'

'The same way you talk to anyone else—with interest and kindness.'

A grudging smile played at the corners of his sardonic mouth. 'Not my style. I'm more into barking orders, Beatriz.'

'Call me Bee…everyone does.'

'No, Bee makes you sound like a maiden aunt. Beatriz is pretty.'

Bee almost winced at that opinion. 'But I'm not.'

'Give the beauty professionals a chance,' Sergios advised without hesitation.

At that advice, Bee took an offended stance, her spine very straight, her chin lifting. 'Actually that's what I wanted to discuss with you.'

With veiled attention, Sergios watched the buttons pull on her shirt, struggling to contain the full globes of her breasts. He wanted to rip open the shirt and release that luscious flesh from captivity into his hands. More than a comfortable handful, he reckoned hungrily, his body hardening. Startled by the imagery, he decided that he had to be in dire need of sexual fulfilment. Clearly he had waited too long to release his desire. He did not want to look on his future wife in that light.

Lost in her own thoughts, Bee breathed in deep and spoke with the abruptness of discomfiture. 'I don't want a makeover. I'm happy as I am. Take me or leave me.'

Sergios was not amused by that invitation. His clever dark eyes rested on her uneasy face. 'You must appreciate that when it comes to your appearance a certain amount of effort is required. Right now, you're making no effort at all.'

Incensed by that critical and wounding statement, Bee threw her slim shoulders back. 'I'm not going to change myself to conform to some outdated sexist code.'

Sergios released an impatient groan. 'Leave the feminism out of it. What's the matter with you? Why don't you care about your appearance?'

'There's nothing the matter with me,' Bee answered with spirit. 'I'm just comfortable with myself as I am.'

'But I'm not. I expect you to smarten up as part of the job.'

'That's too personal a request…beyond your remit,' Bee spelt out in case he hadn't yet got the message. 'I have already given up my home, my job…surely how I choose to look is my business.'

His brilliant dark eyes flamed gold, dense black

lashes lowering over them to enhance the flash-fire effect. 'Not if you want to marry me, it's not.'

Bee flung her head back, glossy chestnut strands trailing across her shoulders, an angry flush across her cheekbones. 'That's ridiculous.'

'Is it? I find you unreasonable. It's normal for a woman to take pride in her appearance. What happened to you that made you lose all interest?' Sergios demanded starkly.

The silence hummed like a buzz saw against Bee's suddenly exposed nerves. She very nearly flinched, for that incisive question had cut deep and hit home hard. There had been a time when Bee had taken great interest in her personal appearance and had chosen her clothes with equal care. But it was not a period she cared to recall. 'I don't want to talk about this. It's absolutely none of your business.'

'The makeover is not negotiable. There will be public occasions when I expect you to appear by my side. There is no longer any excuse for you to go around in unflattering clothes with your hair in a mess,' Sergios asserted with derisive cool.

Rage surged up through Bee like lava seeking a vent. 'How dare you speak to me like that?'

'I'm being honest with you. Come over here,' Sergios urged, a firm hand at her elbow guiding her across to the mirror on the wall. 'And tell me what you see...'

Forced to acknowledge a reflection that displayed windblown hair, an old shirt and baggy jeans, Bee just wanted to slap him. Her teeth gritted. 'It doesn't matter what you say or what you want. I'm not having a makeover and that's that!'

'No makeover, no marriage,' Sergios traded without a second of hesitation. 'It's part of the job and I will not compromise on my expectations.'

Trembling though she was with the force of her emotions, Bee slung him a look of loathing and lifted and dropped her hands in a gesture of finality. 'Then there'll be no marriage because we need to get one thing straight right now, Sergios—'

Sergios lifted a sardonic black brow. 'Do we?'

'You are not going to rule over me like this! You are *not* going to tell me what I do with my hair or what I should wear,' Bee launched back furiously at him, green eyes pure and bright as emeralds in sunshine. 'You're a domineering guy but I won't stand for that.'

Her magnificent bosom was heaving. Was he, at heart, a breast man? he suddenly wondered, questioning his preoccupation with those swelling mounds and seeking an excuse for his strange behaviour. Her eyes were astonishingly vivid in colour. Indeed she looked more attractive in the grip of temper than he had ever seen her but he would not tolerate defiance. 'It is your choice, Beatriz,' Sergios intoned coldly. 'It has always been your choice. At this moment I am having second thoughts about marrying you because you are acting irrationally.'

Assailed by that charge, Bee quivered with sheer fury. '*I'm* being irrational?' she raked back at him incredulously. 'Explain that to me.'

His face set in forbidding lines, Sergios opened the door for her exit instead. 'This discussion is at an end.'

Bee stalked up the stairs in a tempestuous rage. She had never stalked before and she had definitely never been so mad with anger but Sergios Demonides had made her see red. Rot the man, rot him to hell, she thought wildly. How dared he criticise her like that? How dared he ask what had happened to make her lose interest in her appearance? How dared he have that much insight into her actions?

For something traumatic *had* happened to Bee way back when she was madly in love with a man who had ultimately dumped her. That man had replaced her with a little ditsy blonde whose looks and shallow personality had mocked what Bee had once foolishly believed was a good solid relationship. After that devastating wake-up call, the fussing with hair, nails and make-up, not to mention the continual agonising over which outfits were most becoming, had begun to seem utterly superficial, pathetic and a total waste of time. After all, given a free choice Jon had gone for a woman as physically and mentally different from Bee as he could find. For months afterwards, Bee had despised herself for having slavishly followed the girlie code that insisted that a woman's looks were of paramount importance to a man. That code had let her down badly for in spite of all her efforts she had still lost Jon and ever since then she had refused to fuss over her appearance and compete with the true beauties of the world.

And why should she turn herself inside out for Sergios Demonides? He was just like every other man she had met from her father to Jon. Sergios might have briefly flattered her by telling her that she was a loyal daughter and a gifted teacher, but regardless of those qualities he was still judging her by her looks and ready to dump her for failing to meet his standards of feminine beauty. Well, that didn't matter to her, did it?

No, *but* it would certainly matter to her mother, a little voice chimed up quellingly at the back of Bee's brain and she froze in consternation, recalled to reality with a vengeance by that acknowledgement. If Bee backed out of the marriage, Emilia Blake would most probably lose her home, for Bee was convinced that her angry father would try to punish Bee for his failure to get the price he wanted for the Royale hotel group. Monty Blake was that sort of a man. He always needed someone else to blame for his mistakes and losses and Bee and her mother would provide easy targets for his ire.

And if Bee didn't marry Sergios, Paris, Milo and Eleni would suffer yet another adult betrayal. Bee had encouraged the children to bond with her, had announced that she was marrying Sergios and had promised to stay with them. Paris had looked unimpressed but Bee had guessed that he wanted her to prove herself before he took the risk of trusting her. Her sister Zara had already let those children down by winning their acceptance and then vanishing from their lives when she realised that she couldn't go through with marrying their guardian because she had fallen for another man. Was Bee willing to behave in an equally self-centred fashion?

All over the prospect of a visit to a beauty salon and some shopping trips? Wasn't walking out on Sergios because of such trivial activities a case of overkill? He had too much insight though, she acknowledged unhappily. When he had asked her what had happened to her to make her so uninterested in her appearance he had unnerved her and hurt her pride. That was why she had lost her head. He had mortified her when he marched her over to that mirror and forced her to see herself through his eyes. And unhappily Bee had not liked what she saw either. She had seen that her hair needed a decent cut and her wardrobe required an urgent overhaul and that she was being thoroughly unreasonable when she expected a man of his sophistication and faultless grooming to accept her in her current au naturel state.

Bee tidied her hair before descending the stairs at a much more decorous pace than she had raced up them. A mutinous expression tensing her oval face, she lifted a hand as if she was about to knock on the door and then she thought better of the gesture and simply walked back unannounced into his home office.

Sergios was at his desk working on his laptop. His head lifted and glittering dark eyes lit on her, his expression hard and unwelcoming.

It took near physical force for Bee to rise above her hurt pride and part her lips to say, 'All right, I'll do it… the makeover thing.'

'What changed your mind?' Sergios pressed impassively, his expression not softening in the slightest at her capitulation.

'My mother's needs…the children's,' she admitted

truthfully. 'I can't walk out on my responsibilities like that.'

His hard cynical mouth twisted. 'People do it every day.'

Bee stood a little straighter. 'But I don't.'

Sergios pushed away his laptop and rose fluidly upright, astonishingly graceful for a man of his height and powerful build. 'Don't fight me,' he told her huskily. 'I don't like it.'

'But you don't always know best.'

'There are more subtle approaches.' He offered her a drink and she accepted, hovering awkwardly by his desk while she cradled a glass of wine that she didn't really want.

'I'm not sure I do subtle,' Bee confided.

He was suddenly as remote as the Andes. 'You'll learn. I won't be easy to live with.'

And for the first time as she tipped the glass to her lips and tasted an expensive wine as smooth and silky as satin, Bee wondered about Melita. Was he different with his mistress? Was she blonde or brunette? How long had she been in his life? Where did she live? How often did he see her? The torrent of questions blazing a mortifying trail through her head made her redden as she attempted to suppress that flood of unwelcome curiosity. It was none of her business and she didn't care what he did, she told herself squarely. She was to be his wife in name only, nothing more.

'We will drink to our wedding,' Sergios murmured lazily.

'And a better understanding?' Bee completed.

Sergios dealt her a dark appraisal. 'We don't need to understand each other. We won't need to spend that much time together. After a while we won't even have to occupy the same house at the same time…'

Chilled to the marrow by that prediction, Bee drank her wine and set the glass down on the desk. 'Goodnight, then,' she told him prosaically.

And as she climbed the stairs she wondered why she should feel lonelier than she had ever felt in her life before. After all, had she expected Sergios to offer her his company and support? Was he not even prepared to share parenting responsibilities with her? It seemed that in his head the parameters of their relationship were already set in stone: he didn't love her, didn't desire her and, in short, didn't need her except as a mother to the children. Being his wife really would be a job more than anything else…

CHAPTER FOUR

BEE stepped out of the spacious changing cubicle and up onto the dais to get the best possible view of her wedding dress in the mirrored walls of the showroom.

Although it galled her to admit it, Sergios had done astonishingly well. She had had a sharp exchange of words with him when he had startled her with the news that he had actually selected a gown for her.

'What on earth were you thinking of?' Bee had demanded on the phone. 'A woman looks forward to choosing her wedding dress.'

'I was at a fashion show in Milan and the model came down the catwalk in it and I knew immediately that it was *your* dress,' Sergios had drawled with immense assurance.

She had wanted to ask him whom he had accompanied to the fashion show, for she did not believe that he had attended one alone, but she had swallowed back the nosy question. Ignorance, she had decided, was safer than too much information in that department. What she didn't know couldn't hurt her, she told herself staunchly, and not that she was in any danger of being hurt. She could not afford to develop silly notions or possessive feelings towards a man who would not even share a bed with her. Although he had *offered*, she reminded herself darkly, preferring to sacrifice himself if she decided that she could not live without sex rather than allow her to engage in an extra-marital affair.

Now she posed in the wedding gown Sergios had chosen for her, noting how the style showcased her voluptuous cleavage while emphasising her small waist. The neckline was lower than she liked but the fitted bodice definitely flattered her fuller figure. Apparently, Sergios hadn't earned his notorious reputation with women without picking up some useful fashion tips along the way. Bee would have been the first to admit that her appearance had already undergone a major transformation. Her chestnut hair now curved in a sleek layered shoulder-length cut that framed her face, all the heaviness gone. Cosmetics had helped her rediscover her cheekbones and accentuate her best features while every inch of her from her manicured nails to her smooth skin had been waxed, polished and moisturised to as close to perfection as a mortal woman was capable of getting. The irony was that, far from feeling exploited or belittled by the beauty makeover, she was enjoying the energising feel of knowing she looked her very best.

In thirty-six hours it would be her wedding day, Bee acknowledged, breathing in deep and slow to steady her nerves. That afternoon she had a final appointment to sign the pre-nuptial agreement, which had already been explained to her in fine detail during her first visit to the upmarket legal firm employed by Sergios to protect her interests. Her mother's long-term care was comprehensively covered, but she had had to request the right of regular access to the children in the event of their marriage breaking down. Bee was more concerned that Sergios might refuse that demand than she was by the fact that divorce would leave her a wealthy woman. The more time she spent with Paris, Milo and Eleni the more they felt like *her* children.

As Bee left the showroom, elegant in a grey striped dress and light jacket, a bodyguard was by her side and within the space of a minute a limousine was purring up to the kerb to pick her up. She was getting used to being spoilt, she registered guiltily, as she emerged again directly outside the lawyer's plush offices. After only three weeks she was already forgetting what it was like to walk in the rain or queue for a bus.

She was seated in the reception area when she saw a familiar face and she was so shaken by the resulting jolt of recognition that she simply stared, her heartbeat thumping very loudly. It was her ex-boyfriend, Jon Townsend, and more than three years had passed since their last meeting. Now, without the smallest warning, there he was only ten feet away, smartly clad in a business suit and tie. He was slim, dark-haired and attractive, not particularly tall but still taller than she was. As she struggled to overcome her shock she wondered if perhaps he worked for the firm because he had just qualified in law when she first met him.

Jon turned his head and recognised her at almost the same moment as the receptionist invited her to go into Mr Smyth's office. Blue eyes full of surprise, Jon crossed the foyer with a frown. 'Bee?' he queried as though he couldn't quite believe that she was physically there in front of him.

'Jon…sorry, I have an appointment,' Bee responded, rising to her feet.

'You look terrific,' Jon told her warmly.

'Thanks.' Her smile was a mere stretch of her tense lips, for she had not forgotten the pain he had caused her and all her concentration was focused on retaining her dignity. 'Do you work here?'

'Yes, since last year. I'll see you after your appointment and we'll chat,' Jon declared.

Her fake smile dimmed at that disconcerting prospect and she hastened into Halston Smyth's office with a peculiar sense of both relief and anticipation. What could Jon possibly want to chat to her about? It might have happened three long years ago but he *had* ditched her, for goodness' sake. Did they even have any old times to catch up on? Having lost contact with mutual friends after they broke up, she did not think so. He was married now—or at least so she had heard—might even have children, although when she had known him he had not been sure he wanted any. Of course he had been equally unsure he was the marrying kind until he had met Jenna, Bee's little blonde bubbly replacement, the daughter of a high-court judge. A most useful connection for an ambitious young legal whiz-kid, her more cynical self had thought back then.

Mr Smyth ran through the pre-nup again while a more junior member of staff hovered attentively. On her first visit, Bee had realised that as the future wife of a billionaire she was considered big business and they were eager to please. As soon as she realised that her desire to retain contact with the children in the event of a divorce had been incorporated in the agreement, she relaxed. In spite of all the warnings to carefully consider what she was doing she signed on the dotted line while wondering how soon she could book physiotherapy sessions for her mother.

Mr Smyth escorted her all the way to the lift and at the last possible minute before the doors could close Jon stepped in to join her and her bodyguard.

'There's a wine bar round the corner,' Jon informed her casually.

Her brow furrowed. 'I'm not sure we have much to talk about.'

'Well, I can't physically persuade you to join me with a security man in tow,' he quipped with a familiar grin.

'Do you know this gentleman, Miss Blake?' her bodyguard, Tom, asked, treating Jon to an openly suspicious appraisal.

Meeting Jon's amused look, Bee almost giggled. 'Yes. Yes, I do,' she confirmed. 'I can't stay long, though.'

Curiosity had to be behind his request, Bee decided. After all, three years ago when Jon had been with her she had been a final-year student teacher from a fairly ordinary background. While her father might be wealthy, Bee had never enjoyed a personal allowance or, aside of the occasional family invite, an entrée into Monty Blake's exclusive world. Jon was most probably aware that she was on the brink of marrying one of the richest men in Europe and wondering how that had come about. She suppressed a rueful smile over the awareness that few people would believe the truth behind that particular development.

In the bar her bodyguard chose a seat nearby and talked on his phone. Jon ordered drinks and made light conversation. She remembered when his smile had made her tummy tighten and her heart beat a little faster and crushed the recollection.

'Jenna and I got a divorce a couple of months ago,' Jon volunteered wryly.

'I'm sorry to hear that,' Bee said uncomfortably.

'It was an infatuation.' Jon pulled a rueful face. 'I lived to regret leaving you.'

'Never mind about that now. I don't hold grudges,' Bee interposed, feeling a shade awkward beneath the earnest onslaught of his blue eyes.

'That's pretty decent of you. Now let me get to the point of my invite and you are, of course, welcome to tell me that I'm a calculating so-and-so!' Jon teased, extracting a leaflet from his pocket and passing it across the table to her. 'I would be very grateful if you would consider becoming a patron for this charity. It does a lot of good work and could do with the support.'

Bee was taken aback, for the Jon she recalled had been too intent on climbing the career ladder to spend time raising money for good causes. Maturity, it seemed, had made him a more well-rounded person and she was impressed. He was a trustee for a charity for disabled children, similar to one she had volunteered with when she was a student. 'I doubt that I could do much on a personal basis because I'll be based in Greece after the wedding.'

'As the wife of Sergios Demonides, your name alone would be sufficient to generate a higher profile for the organisation,' Jon assured her with enthusiasm. 'And if you were to decide to get more involved the occasional appearance at public events would be very welcome.'

Bee was relieved then that it appeared Jon's desire to see her was professional rather than personal. She very much appreciated the fact that he studiously avoided asking her anything about Sergios. They parted fifteen minutes later but before she could turn away, Jon reached for her hand.

'I meant what I said earlier,' he stressed in an undertone. 'I made a colossal mistake. I've always regretted losing you, Bee.'

Green eyes turning cool, Bee was quick to retrieve her hand. 'It's a little late in the day to tell me that, Jon.'

'I hope you'll be happy with Demonides.' But the look on his face told her that he didn't think she would be.

Unsettled by that exchange, Bee travelled back to Sergios's house to have tea with the children. Sergios had been jetting round the world on business for over two weeks and their only contact had been by phone. After their meal Bee supervised Paris's homework assignment and bathed Milo and Eleni before tucking them into bed. In a month's time, Eleni was scheduled for surgery to have grommets inserted in both ears to resolve her hearing problems. Having consulted Paris's teacher, Bee had learned that the boy was struggling to make friends at school and she had tried to improve the situation by inviting some of his classmates over to play after school. Paris was beginning to find his feet and as he did so he had become more receptive to Bee and less suspicious of her.

Just before Bee went to bed, Sergios called from Tokyo. 'Who was the man you accompanied to the wine bar?' he demanded.

Bee stiffened defensively. 'So, Tom's a spy, is he?'

'Beatriz…' Sergios growled impatiently, forceful as a lion roaring a warning to an unwary prey.

'He was just an old friend I hadn't seen since university.' Bee hesitated but decided to say nothing more, feeling she didn't owe Sergios any more of an explanation.

'You'll find that plenty of old friends will come scurrying out of the woodwork now that you're marrying me,' Sergios replied cynically.

'I find that offensive. This particular friend is asking me to get involved with a children's charity. You can scarcely find fault with that.'

'Is that why he was holding hands with you?'

Bee flushed scarlet. 'He grasped my hand—big deal!'

'In public places I expect you to be discreet.'

Her anger rose. 'You always have to have the last word, don't you?'

'And I'm always right, *latria mou*,' Sergios agreed equably, not one whit disturbed by the accusation.

That night Bee lay in her big luxurious bed and played the game of 'what if' with Jon in a starring role.

Well, she was only human and naturally she could not help wondering what might have happened had she met her charming ex when she was not on the brink of getting married to another man. Probably nothing would have happened, she decided ruefully, for had it not been for the pressure Sergios had put on her she would have looked like a real Plain Jane and Jon would have been less than impressed. In any case, Sergios was much better looking and had a great deal more personality…

Now where on earth had that thought come from? Bee wondered in confusion. There was no denying that Sergios was a very, very handsome guy but he was not *her* guy in the way Jon had once seemed to be and he never would be. Bee decided that she was far too sensible to indulge in 'what if' dreams. Besides she had long since worked out that if Jon had truly loved her he would never have dumped her because she had a mother who would always need her support. Jon's rejection had shattered the dream of family, which Bee valued most.

'That's a very romantic dress,' Tawny commented, studying her half-sister with frankly curious eyes, for the fitted lace gown with the flowing skirt was exceedingly feminine and not in Bee's usual conservative style. 'And a very thoughtful choice for a guy entering a very practical marriage of convenience.'

Bee went pink, wishing her other sister, Zara, had not been quite so frank with their youngest sister, who thoroughly disapproved of what Bee was doing in marrying a man she didn't love. She also wished Zara had not chosen to avoid what might have been an uncomfortable occasion for her by pleading her reluctance to travel while pregnant. 'Sergios isn't romantic and neither am I.'

'Granted the kids are cute,' Tawny conceded, her coppery head held at a considering angle, blue eyes troubled. 'And Sergios, on the outside he's sex on a stick, but only for an adventurous woman and you're as conventional as they come.'

'You never know,' Bee quipped, lifting her bouquet.

'If I was the suspicious type I would suspect that you're doing this for your mother's benefit,' Tawny commented with a frown, revealing a glimpse of wits that were sharp as a knife. 'You'd do anything for her and she's a lovely woman.'

'Yes, isn't she? My mother is also very happy for me today,' Bee slotted in with a pointed glance. 'Please don't spoil that for her by giving her the wrong idea about my marriage...'

'Or even the *right* idea,' Tawny muttered half under her breath, not being that easy to silence. 'Just promise me that if he's awful to live with you'll divorce him.'

Bee nodded instant agreement to soothe her half-sibling's concerns and descended the stairs with care in her high heels. She was in her mother's house for she had spent the last night of her single life there at the older woman's request. Tawny was not acting as a bridesmaid because Bee had drawn the line at taking the masquerade of her wedding that far.

'But I know you, you won't do it if it means leaving those cute kids behind.' Tawny sighed. 'You'll be like faithful Penelope, stuck with him for ever, and I bet he plays on it when he realises what a softy you are.'

Bee had no intention of being a pushover, convinced as she was that Sergios would happily tread a softy right into the ground and walk on without a backward glance. He was tough, so she had to be even tougher. She reminded herself of that fact when her scowling father extended his arm to her at the mouth of the church aisle and fixed a social smile to his face. Monty Blake had recently been trodden on by Sergios and his ego and his pockets were still stinging from the encounter. She thought it said even more about Sergios's intimidating influence that her father was still willing, however, to play his part at their wedding.

Full of impatience, Sergios wheeled round at the altar to watch his bride approach. His face unreadable, he studied her and started to frown. She had had her long hair cut back to her shoulders. Whose very stupid idea had that been? But aside from that, Beatriz looked… luscious, he finally selected after a long mental pause while he ran his brooding dark gaze from the sultry peach-tinted fullness of her mouth down to the generous curves he never failed to admire. He wondered absently if men developed a taste for larger breasts when they reached a certain age. He was thirty-two, not fifty-two though. But as he saw the burgeoning swell of those plump creamy mounds so beautifully displayed in that neckline there was no denying that he was spellbound. The model on the catwalk in Milan had had nothing to show off but an expanse of flat bony chest. In her place, however, Beatriz would have been a show-stopper. He frowned at that thought.

Determined not to be cowed by the fact her bridegroom was glowering at her, Bee lifted her chin. Even the most critical woman would have had to admit that Sergios did look spectacularly handsome in a beautifully cut morning suit. Encountering those hard eyes trained on her, she felt briefly dizzy and breathless. The minister of her church was inclined to ramble a little, but he soon controlled the tendency after Sergios urged him in an impatient undertone to 'speed it up'. Affronted by her bridegroom's intervention, Bee reddened to the roots of her hair. Had Sergios no idea how to behave in church? Well, it was never too late for a man to learn, although she suspected he would fight learning anything from her every step of the way. He thrust the wedding ring onto her finger with scant ceremony. She rubbed her hand as though he had hurt her, although he had not.

'You were rude to the minister,' she said on the way down the aisle again.

A brow lifted. 'I beg your pardon?'

'You heard me. There are some occasions when you just have to be patient for the sake of good manners and a wedding service is one of those occasions.'

In the thunderous silence that now enfolded the bridal couple, Milo wriggled like an eel off his nanny's lap and rushed to Bee's side to clutch her skirt. She patted his curly head to quieten him and took his hand in hers.

'He was repeating himself,' Sergios breathed harshly,

but, watching the toddler beam his big trusting smile up at Bee, he restrained the outrage her impertinence had sent hurtling through him. After little more than two weeks abroad he had returned to his London home and noticed a distinct change for the better in his cousin Timon's children. All the kids had calmed down. Milo had become less frantic in his need for attention, the little girl was smiling and even Paris was occasionally venturing into shy speech.

Sergios had never had a best friend but had he done so Timon would have come the closest, although on the surface serious, steady and quiet Timon would have appeared to have had little in common with Sergios's altogether more aggressive extrovert nature. But the bond had been there all the same and it was a matter of honour to Sergios to see Timon's children thrive in his care. Beatriz, it seemed, had the magic touch in that department.

A line of cameras greeted their emergence from the church. As Bee's eyes widened and she froze with the dismay of someone unaccustomed to media attention Sergios took immediate advantage of the moment. He swung her round into the circle of his arms and, with one hand braced to the shallow indentation of her spine to draw her close, he bent his head and kissed her, instinctively righting the status quo in the only way available to him.

Shock crashed through Bee and made her knees shake at that first breath-taking instant of physical contact. She had never been less prepared for anything and impressions hit her in a flood of overwhelming sensuality: the exotic tang of his designer cologne, the uncompromising strength and power of that lean, muscular body crushing her softer curves, the hard, demanding pressure of his erotic mouth on hers. And while at the back of her mind a voice was shrieking no and urging her to pull back her body was singing entirely another song. There was a wildly addictive fire to the taste of him. She wanted more, she wanted *so* much more she trembled with the astonishing force of that wanting. His raw masculine passion sliced through her every defence and roused a surge of naked hunger within her. The plunge of his tongue into the sensitive interior of her mouth made her body tremble, while heat pooled between her thighs and her breasts swelled, pushing against the lace of her bra so that it felt too tight for comfort.

'You're not supposed to taste that good, *yineka mou*,' Sergios breathed in a roughened undertone, drawing back, his brilliant dark eyes cloaked and cool, his face taut.

Dragging her clinging hands from his broad shoulders, Bee was aghast and she turned blindly to pose for the cameras, her head swimming, her treacherous body torn by silent anguish as she struggled to suppress that monstrous hunger he had awakened. She had never felt like that in her life before, not even with Jon. It was as if Sergios had called up something she hadn't known existed within her and that treacherous loss of control had embarrassed the hell out of her. My goodness, she had *clung* to him, pushed her breasts into his chest like a wanton hussy and kissed him back with far too much gusto. She could not bring herself to look at him again and inside she was dying of mortification. Obviously he had planned to give her a social kiss for the benefit of the cameras but she had flung herself into it as though she were sex-starved.

Teeth gritted behind his determined smile, Sergios willed his arousal into subjugation and reminded himself forcefully that sleeping with his wife would curtail his freedom and deprive him of the choices that any intelligent man would value. One woman was much like another; all cats were grey in the dark. He repeated that oft-considered mantra to himself with rigorous determination: he had no plans to bed his bride, no need to do so either. To think otherwise was to invite chaos into his head and home. Breaking the rules of his marriage would cost him and why take that risk? Unless he was very much mistaken, and when the subject was women Sergios was rarely mistaken, his mistress would push out every sexual stop to impress him on his next visit. Satisfaction could be had without complications and wasn't that all that really mattered?

The reception was staged at an exclusive hotel where security staff vetted every arriving guest.

'Zara was such a fool,' Bee's stepmother, Ingrid Blake, remarked in her brittle voice. 'It could have been her standing here in your place today.'

Features austere, Sergios settled an arm to his bride's rigid spine. 'There can be no comparison. Beatriz is...special,' he murmured huskily.

Bee went pink at the unexpected compliment, although the apparent slur on Zara embarrassed her and as the older woman moved out of earshot Bee muttered, 'Ingrid has a wasp's tongue but I could have managed her on my own.'

'I will never stand in silence while my wife is being insulted,' Sergios asserted. 'But only the most foolish would risk incurring my wrath.'

'Ingrid is a sourpuss but she's my father's wife and a member of the family,' Bee reminded him gently.

Noting the anxious light in her gaze, Sergios laughed out loud. 'You can't protect everyone from me.'

His vital laugh, so full of his essential energy, ironically chilled her, reminding her how much ruthless power and influence he had in the world and how much he took it for granted. She thought of her father walking her down the aisle even though it would have been more in character for the older man to express his resentment by refusing to take part in the wedding. Monty Blake's submission to her husband's wishes had shaken Bee and shown her the meaning of true supremacy. She had no doubt that if she ever dared to cross Sergios he would become her most bitter enemy.

'I understood that your grandfather was planning to come today,' Bee admitted.

'He has bronchitis and his doctor advised him to stay at home. You'll meet him tomorrow when we arrive in Greece. I didn't want him to take the risk of travelling.'

It was not a particularly large wedding: Sergios equated small with the privacy and discretion with which he liked to separate his private life from his public one. Although there were only fifty guests everybody on Sergios's list was a *somebody* in the business world. He seemed to have very few actual relatives, explaining that his grandfather had had only two children, both of whom had died relatively young.

'Was he looking for an heir when he discovered you?'

'No. In those days he had Timon. Social services discovered my connection to Nectarios and informed him about me. He didn't know I even existed before that. He came to see me when I was seventeen. I needed a decent education, he offered the opportunity,' Sergios admitted tautly.

She wanted to ask him more about his parentage but his reluctance to discuss his background was obvious and it seemed neither the time nor the place to probe further. Tense at being so much the centre of attention, she ate a light meal. A celebrity group entertained them. Bee noticed a beautiful female guest casting lascivious eyes in Sergios's direction and felt her fingers flex like claws ready to scratch. She didn't like other women looking at him in that speculative sexual way as if trying to imagine what he would be like in bed. It was that wretched kiss, it had changed everything, even the way she thought about him, Bee conceded unhappily.

She had not known that a mere kiss could make her feel hot and hungry and frantic for another. In fact she had always believed that she wasn't that sexual, and even when she was in love with Jon keeping him at arm's length had not proved much of a challenge for her. She had longed for some sign of commitment from him before she slept with him, had wanted sexual intimacy to mean something beyond the physical. With hindsight she suspected that she had always sensed that

Jon was holding back as well and reluctant to get in too deep with her.

'This day seems endless,' Sergios breathed tersely as he checked his phone for the hundredth time, fingers tapping a restive tattoo on the table.

'It'll be over soon,' Bee said calmly, for she had guessed at the church that he found almost every aspect of their wedding day a demanding challenge. It made her wonder what his first wedding and his first wife had been like. Was he reliving disturbing memories? Had his first wedding been a day of love and joy for him? How could she not wonder? Yet Sergios didn't strike her as the kind of guy likely to have buried his heart with his dead wife and unborn child in the grave eight years earlier. He was too pragmatic and abrasive and far too fond of female company.

'Let's get the dancing over with,' Sergios breathed abruptly, springing upright and extending a hand to her.

'I love your enthusiasm,' Bee riposted, smiling brightly as her mother beamed at her. Emilia Blake was a happy woman and Sergios had not only visited her before the wedding but had also made the effort to sit down and talk that afternoon to her, which Bee appreciated. Emilia believed that her son-in-law was the sun, the moon and the stars and not for worlds would Bee have done or said anything to detract from that positive impression.

This marriage *had* to work, she reflected anxiously. If her mother came out to live in Greece their relationship would be on constant display, so she had to ensure from the start that the marriage worked for both of them. She would have to be practical, even-tempered and tolerant...for he was neither of the last two things. Sergios shifted his lean powerful length against her as he danced with a fine sense of rhythm and all those rational uplifting thoughts left her head in one bound for suddenly all she was conscious of were the tightening prominence of her nipples and the smouldering dark gold of his eyes as he gazed moodily down at her. Heat and butterflies rose and fluttered in the pit of her tummy. Desire, she recognised as the twisty sensation stirring up hunger in her pelvis, was digging talon claws of need into her.

'*Theos*...you move well,' Sergios husked, whirling her round and admiring both her energy and the pert stirring curve of her derriere as she wriggled it in time to the music.

'After years of dance classes, I ought to.'

From there the day seemed to speed up. Moving from table to table, group to group, they spoke to all their guests. Bee was impressed that Sergios put on such a good show. He did not strike her as a touchy-feely guy, but the whole time he was by her side he maintained physical contact with either an arm or a hand placed on her. The children got tired and the nannies took them back to the house. Within an hour of their departure Sergios decided they could leave as well and they climbed into a waiting limousine and were carried off. From below her feathery lashes, Bee glanced covertly at her new husband, recognising his relief that the occasion was over.

'Is it all weddings you don't like or just your own?'

'All of them,' he admitted, his handsome mouth hardening. 'I can't stand the starry eyes and the unrealistic expectations. It's not real life.'

'No, it's hope and there's nothing wrong with the fact that people long for a happy ending.'

Sergios shrugged a big broad shoulder in what struck her as the diplomatic silence of disagreement. He sprawled back into the corner of the leather seat, long powerful thighs splayed in relaxation. 'Do you long for a happy ending, Beatriz?'

'Why not?' Bee fielded lightly.

'It won't be with me,' he promised her grimly. 'I don't believe in them.'

Well, that was certainly telling her, she thought ruefully as the limo drew up outside the London house that had become her new home. They mounted the splendid staircase together and were traversing the landing to head off in different directions when Sergios turned to Bee, his face impassive. 'I'm getting changed and going out. I'll see you at the airport tomorrow.'

And with that concluding assurance delivered with the minimum of drama he strode down the corridor where his bedroom suite lay and vanished from view. A door thudded shut. Bee had fallen still and she was very pale. She felt as if he had punched her in the stomach, winding her so that she couldn't catch her breath. It was the first day of their marriage, their wedding night, and he was going out, leaving her at home on her own.

And why should he not? This was not a normal marriage, she reminded herself doggedly. It was not his duty to keep her company, was it? But was he going to see another woman? Why should that idea bite as if an arrow tipped with acid had been fired into her flesh? She didn't know why, she only knew it hurt and she felt horribly rejected. It felt humiliating to ask one of the maids for her assistance in getting out of her wedding finery. Yet, she knew that had he even been available she would not have approached Sergios for the same help. Still feeling gutted and furious with herself for a reaction she could not understand, Bee went for a shower to remove the last remnants of bridal sparkle from her body. Sergios wasn't her husband, not really her husband, so what was the matter with her?

Did Melita live in London or was she here visiting for a prearranged meeting? Or could it be that Sergios was rendezvousing with some other woman? Presumably he would be having sex with someone else tonight. Her tummy muscles tightened as if in self-defence and perspiration dampened her brow, leaving her skin clammy. There was no point being prudish or naive about the emptiness of her marriage, she told herself in exasperation. Right from the start Sergios had demanded the freedom to get naked and intimate with other women on a regular basis. According to the media and those ladies who, when he was younger, were anything but discreet about his habits in the bedroom, he was very highly sexed.

And what exactly did she have to complain about? Sergios was doing only what he had said he would do and by loathing what he was doing *she* was the one breaking the rules by getting too personally involved! It was time she was more honest with herself, she reasoned irritably. In the normal way a man of Sergios's dazzling good looks and wealth would never be attracted to a woman as ordinary as she was. She should not forget that his first wife, Krista, had been gorgeous, similar to Zara with her fragile blonde loveliness. Bee had won Sergios as a husband solely by agreeing to allow him to retain his freedom within the marriage and be a mother to his cousin's children. That was how it was and that was the reality that she had to learn to live with.

A knock sounded on the door and she called out. Paris, clad in his superhero pyjamas and slippers, peered in, a photo album tucked snugly beneath one arm. 'I saw Uncle Sergios going out. Do you want to see my photos?'

'Why not?' Bee said with resolute good cheer, for a regular appraisal of photos of his parents and his baby years had become quite a feature of the little boy's life in recent days. He would show Bee the pictures and explain who the people were and where and when he thought they were taken and she would *ooh* and *aah* with appreciation and ask questions while he worked through his sadness for a period of his life that was now gone.

'Would you like a hot drink to help you sleep?' she prompted, deciding that this was a wedding night that she would never forget.

And if Bee blinked back tears while she sat on the side of her bed with an arm anchored comfortingly round Paris's skinny little body and a mug of cocoa in her other hand, her companion was too intent on sharing his photo album to notice.

CHAPTER FIVE

Two nannies, Janey and Karen, were accompanying Bee and the children to Greece. Shown around Sergios's incredibly large and opulent private jet by an attentive stewardess late the next morning, Bee saw the entire party settled in the rear cabin, which was separate from the main saloon. Armed with enough toys, magazines and films to while away a much longer flight, the young women were thrilled by their deluxe surroundings.

In a lighter mood, Bee would have found it equally difficult not to be seduced by her newly luxurious mode of travel, but she had too much on her mind. She had slept badly and had been forced to out-act a Hollywood film star with her good cheer over the breakfast table, for she had been keen to soothe the boys' nervous tension. After all, Paris and Milo were apprehensive about making yet another move for they had already had to adjust to so much change in their short lives. Paris, however, was quick to address the steward in Greek and Milo's head tipped to one side and his brow furrowed as though he too was recalling the language of his very first words. Although they would not be returning to their former home in Athens, they were heading back to the country of their birth and they might well find Sergios's home on the island of Orestos familiar, for they had often visited it with their parents.

Having ensured that everyone was comfortable, Bee returned to the main saloon and took a seat to leaf through a magazine that she couldn't have cared less about. Having teamed a green silk top and cardigan with white linen trousers, she felt both smart and comfortable. Her hand shook a little when she heard voices outside and her fingers clenched tightly into the publication in her hand, her body tensing, her heartbeat literally racing as she heard steps on the metal stairs. Sergios was tearing her in two, she suddenly thought in frustration. One half of her could barely wait to lay eyes on him while the other half would have preferred to never see him again.

'Kalimera…good morning, Beatriz,' Sergios intoned, as tall, dark and gloriously handsome as an angel come to earth, perfect in form but exceedingly complex in nature.

And with her breath convulsing in her dry throat, she both looked at him and blanked him at one and the same time so that their eyes did not quite meet, a polite smile of acknowledgement on her lips combined with an almost inaudible greeting. Why was she embarrassed? Why the hell was she embarrassed? Enraged by her ridiculous oversensitivity, Bee glanced up at him unwarily and collided with golden eyes full of energy and wariness. She *knew* it, he was no fool, and indeed he was just waiting for her to say or do something she shouldn't, to react in some inappropriate way to his departure the night before. Keeping her smile firmly in place, Bee was determined to deny him that satisfaction and she dropped her attention resolutely back to her magazine.

And there her attention stayed…throughout take-off, a visit to the children, lunch and the remainder of the flight. Sergios shot her composed profile a suspicious appraisal. She had said not one word out of place, not one word. He could not understand why he was not pleased by the fact, why indeed he felt almost affronted by her comprehensive show of disinterest and detachment. He did not like and had even less experience of being ignored by a woman. But Beatriz was very much a lady and he appreciated that trait. The acknowledgement sparked a recollection and he dug into his pocket to remove a jewel box.

'For you,' he murmured carelessly, tossing the little box down on the table between them.

Her teeth gritted. She lifted the box almost as though she were afraid it might soil her in some way, flipped up the lid, stared down at the fabulous diamond solitaire ring, closed the lid and set it aside again. 'Thank you,' she pronounced woodenly with anything but gratitude in her low-pitched voice.

Too clever not to work out that the denial of attention was some form of challenge and punishment, Sergios was becoming tenser because his brand-new bride was already revealing murky depths he had not known she possessed. Frustration filled him. Why did women *do* that? Why did they pretend to be straightforward and then welch on the deal with a vengeance? He knew she was strong-willed, stubborn and rather set in her conventional ways but he had not foreseen any greater problem and had by his own yardstick done what he could to cement their relationship.

'Aren't you going to put it on?' Sergios prompted flatly.

Bee opened the box again, removed the ring and rammed it roughly down over the third finger of her right hand with a lack of ceremony or appreciation that was even more challenging than her previous behaviour. She then returned to perusing her magazine with renewed concentration. She was so furious with him she could neither trust herself to speak to or look at him. If she did look, she would only end up picturing him cavorting in a messy tangle of bed sheets with some sinuous, sexy lover to whom she could never compare in looks or appeal. Yet until that very day looks or sex appeal had never seemed that important to Bee, who had been happier to put a higher value on her health and peace of mind. Unfortunately marrying Sergios appeared to have destroyed her peace of mind.

After a long moment of disbelief, for no woman had ever accepted a gift from him with such incivility before, dark temper stirred in Sergios. Simmering, he studied her, catching the jewelled glint of defiance in her green eyes as she sneaked a glance at him from below her curling lashes and bent her head. Shining chestnut hair fell against the flawless creamy skin of her cheek and her voluptuous pink mouth compressed. That fast he went taut and hard, sexual heat leaving him swallowing back a curse under his breath as he imagined what she might do with those full pouting lips if he got her in the right mood, and Sergios had never once doubted his ability to get a woman in the right mood.

'Excuse me,' Bee said without expression, breaking the tense silence. She was on her feet before he was even aware she was about to move. Seconds later she disappeared into the rear cabin and he heard Milo yell out her name in welcome.

Almost light-headed with relief at escaping the fraught atmosphere in the saloon, Bee sat down to amuse the children. The younger nanny, Janey, caught her hand and gasped at the huge diamond on her finger. 'That ring is out of this world, Mrs Demonides!' she exclaimed, impressed to death.

No, that ring is the price of lust, Bee could have told her. Bee was deeply insulted. He had had sex with another woman and it had meant so little to him that he had betrayed not a shred of discomfiture in Bee's presence. He was, as always, beautifully dressed and immaculate without even a hint of another woman's lipstick or perfume on him. That he was as cool as ice as well offended her sense of decency. She had wanted to throw that ring back at him and tell him to keep it. She had had to leave the saloon before she did or said something that she would live to regret.

Why couldn't she start thinking of him as a brother or a friend? Why was she burdened with this awful sense of possessiveness where Sergios was concerned? Why did she have to be so hatefully attracted to him? It was an appalling admission to make but she already knew that she couldn't bear the idea of Sergios with another woman in an intimate situation. Had she developed some kind of silly immature crush on him? She cringed at the suspicion but what else could be causing all these distressingly unsuitable feelings?

She had to reprogramme her brain to view him in the light of a brother, an asexual being, she instructed herself firmly. That was the only way forward in their relationship. That was the only way their marriage of convenience could possibly work for all of them. She had her mother's happiness to think about as well as that of Paris, Milo and Eleni. This marriage was not all about *her* and her very personal reactions to Sergios were a dangerous trap that she could not afford to fall into.

After all, Sergios was not all bad. He was tough, ruthless, arrogant and selfish, but while he might have the morals of an alley cat he had been remarkably kind to her mother. Without even being asked to do so, he had behaved as though theirs was a normal marriage for Emilia Blake's benefit. Although he appeared to have little interest in his cousin's kids or kids in general, he had still retained guardianship of the troubled trio and had married Bee on their behalf. Yet he could more easily have shirked the responsibility and retained his freedom by paying someone else to do the job of raising them for him.

The jet landed in Athens and the entire party transferred to a large helicopter to travel to the island of Orestos. Conscious of the cool gleam in Sergios's appraisal, Bee went pink and pretended not to notice while peering out of the windows to get a clear view of the island that was to be her future home. Orestos was craggy and green with a hilly interior. Pine forests backed white sand beaches that ran down to a violet blue shining sea and a sizeable small town surrounded the harbour.

'Gorgeous, just like a postcard!' one of the nannies commented admiringly.

'Has the island been in your family for long?' Bee asked Sergios.

'My great-grandfather accepted it in lieu of a bad debt in the nineteen twenties.'

'It looks like a wonderfully safe place for children to run about,' the other nanny remarked approvingly to her companion.

Bee thought of the far from safe and tough inner city streets where Sergios had grown up. Perhaps it was not that surprising that he was so hard and uncompromising in his attitude to the world and the people in it, she conceded reluctantly. The helicopter landed on a pad within yards of a big white house adorned with a tall round tower. Surrounded by the pine forest, it could not be seen except from the air. Sergios jumped out and spun round to help her leave the craft. Laughing uproariously in excitement, Milo jumped out too and would have run off had Sergios not clamped a restraining hand into the collar of his sweatshirt.

'There are dangers here with such easy access to the sea and the rocks,' he informed the hovering nannies. 'Don't let the boys leave the house alone.'

The warning killed the bubbly holiday atmosphere that had been brewing, Bee noted. Janey and Karen looked intimidated.

'The children are going to love it here but they'll have to learn new rules to keep them safe,' Bee forecast, stepping into the uneasy silence.

The housekeeper, Androula, a plump, good-natured woman with a beaming smile, came out to welcome them with a stream of Greek. Sergios came to a sudden halt as if something she had said had greatly surprised him.

'Nectarios is here,' he said in a sudden aside, his ebony brows drawing together in a frown.

'I assumed that your grandfather lived with you.'

'No, he has his own house across the bay. Androula tells me that his home suffered a flood during a rain storm, rendering it uninhabitable,' he said with the suggestion of gritted teeth. 'This changes everything.'

Bee had no idea what he was talking about. Androula swept them indoors and a tall, broad-shouldered and eagle-eyed elderly man came out to meet them. Paris rushed eagerly straight to his white-haired great-grandfather's side, Milo trailing trustingly in his brother's wake. Keen dark eyes set below beetling brows rested on Bee and she flushed, feeling hugely self-conscious.

'Introduce me to your bride, Sergios,' the old man encouraged. 'I'm sorry to invade your privacy at such a time.'

'You're family. You will always be a welcome guest here,' Bee declared warmly, some of the strain etched in her face dissipating. 'Look how pleased the boys are to see you.'

'Beauty and charm,' Nectarios remarked softly to his grandson. 'You've done well, Sergios.'

Bee did not think she was beautiful, but she thought it was very kind of the old man to pretend otherwise. At that very moment her make-up had worn off and she was wearing creased linen trousers stained by Milo's handprints. Eleni was whinging and stretching out her arms to her and she took the child and rested her against her shoulder, smoothing her little dark head to soothe her. The children were getting tired and cross and she took advantage of the fact to leave the men and follow Androula to the nursery. While the boys enthused over toys familiar from previous visits, Bee asked Androula to show her to her room. Her accommodation was in the tower and her eyes opened very wide when she entered the huge circular bedroom with full-height French windows opening out onto a stone balcony with the most fabulous view of the bay. It was a spectacular and comparatively new addition to the house and her eyes only opened wider when she was taken through the communicating door to inspect a luxurious en suite and matching dressing rooms. Purpose-built accommodation for two and her cheeks warmed. Naturally the household would be expecting Sergios and his bride to share this amazing suite of rooms.

Assured that she had time before dinner, Bee scooped up the wrap she glimpsed in one of her open cases and left the maids to unpack while she went for a bath. She was just in the mood to soak away her stress. Leaving her clothes in an unusually untidy heap and anchoring her hair to the top of her head to keep it dry, she tossed scented bath crystals into the water and climbed in, sinking down into the relaxing warmth with a sigh of appreciation.

A knock sounded on the door and she frowned, recalling that she had not locked it. She was in the act of sitting up when the door opened without further warning to frame Sergios.

Bee whipped her arms over her breasts and roared, 'Get out of here!'

'No, I will not,' Sergios responded with thunderous bite.

CHAPTER SIX

THE smouldering gold of anger in Sergios's stunning eyes dimmed solely because he was enjoying the view.

There Beatriz was, all pink and wet and bare among the bubbles. Her fair skin was all slippery and his hands tingled with the need to touch. Those breasts he had correctly calculated at more than a handful were topped by buds with the size and lushness of ripe cherries. Erect at that tempting vision within seconds, Sergios was deciding that the need to share facilities might not be quite the serious problem and invasion of privacy that he had gloomily envisaged. In fact it might well pay unexpected dividends of a physical nature.

Outraged green eyes seethed at him. 'Go!' Bee yelled at him.

Instead, Sergios stepped into the bathroom and closed the door to lean back against the wood with infuriating cool. 'Don't raise your voice to me. The maids are unpacking next door and we're supposed to be on our honeymoon,' he reminded her huskily. 'For someone so hung up on good manners you can be very rude. I knocked on the door—you chose not to answer!'

'You didn't give me the chance.' Bee said resentfully

before she reached for a towel, fed up with huddling like some cowed Victorian maiden in the water and all too well aware that her hands didn't cover a large enough expanse of flesh to conceal the more sensitive areas. As she got up on her knees she deftly used the towel as cover and slowly stood up, keen not to expose anything more.

Fully appreciating the rolling violin curve visible between her waist and hip, Sergios treated her to a wolfish grin of amusement. 'You need a bigger towel, Beatriz.'

And just like that Beatriz became instantly aware of the fact she was large and clumsy rather than little and dainty. Equally fast she was recalling her size zero sister, Zara, whom Sergios had initially planned to marry, not to mention his equally tiny first wife. That was the shape of woman that was the norm for her Greek husband. On his terms she *was* a big girl.

'Or you could just drop the towel altogether, *yineka mou*,' Sergios continued huskily, his dark deep drawl roughening round the edges at that prospect.

'If I wasn't so busy trying to knot this stupid towel I would slap you!' Beatriz countered, assuming that he was teasing her, for by no stretch of the imagination could she even picture circumstances in which she might deliberately stand naked in front of a man, even if he was the one whom she had married.

Sergios tossed her a much larger towel from the shelf on the wall and she wrapped it round her awkwardly. 'We have to share this suite,' he spelt out, suddenly serious.

Her brow indented. 'What are you talking about?'

'My grandfather is staying and I want him to believe that this is a normal marriage. He won't believe that if we occupy separate rooms and behave like brother and sister,' he said with a sardonic curl to his wide sensual mouth. 'We don't have a choice. We'll just have to tough it out and hope our acting skills are up to the challenge.'

'You're expecting me to share that bedroom with you...even *the bed*?' Bee gasped. 'I won't do it.'

'I didn't offer you a choice. We have an arrangement and it includes providing cover for each other.' Eyes dramatised by black spiky lashes raked her truculent face in an unashamed challenge. 'We do what we have to do. I don't want to upset Nectarios just as you didn't want to worry your mother. He needs to believe that this is a real marriage.'

'But I am not willing to agree to share a bed with you,' Bee repeated with clarity. 'And that's all I've got to say on the subject apart from the fact that if you sleep out there, I'll have to sleep somewhere else.'

His eyes glittered as bright as stars in the night sky. 'Not under my roof—'

Bee felt somewhat foolish and at a disadvantage swaddled in her unflattering towel for if she looked large without it how much larger must she look engulfed within its capacious folds? And had a towel the size of a blanket been a deliberate choice on his part or a coincidence?

'I'll get dressed for dinner,' Bee announced, waiting for him to step aside and let her out of the bathroom. *Not under my roof?* He could be as threatening as a sabre-toothed tiger but she was not about to change her mind: she was entitled to her own bed.

Eyes narrowed with brooding intensity, Sergios lounged back against the door frame like the lean, powerful predator that he was and the atmosphere was explosive. As she moved past he rested a hand on the bare curve of her shoulder and she came to a halt.

'I want you,' Sergios declared, using his other hand to ease her back against him and run his fingers lightly up from her waist to her ribcage.

In the space of a moment Bee froze and stopped breathing, panic gripping her. *I want you?* Since when?

'That's not part of our agreement,' she said prosaically, standing as still as a statue as if movement of any kind might encourage him.

Above her head, Sergios laughed, the sound full of vitality and amusement. 'Our agreement is between adults and whatever we choose to make of it—'

'Trust me,' Bee urged. 'We don't want to muddy the water with sex.'

'This is the real world. Desire is an energy, not something you can plan or pin down on paper,' he intoned, and his hands simply shifted position to cover her towel-clad breasts.

Even beneath that light pressure, her heartbeat went crazy. Boom-boom-boom it went in her ears as he boldly pushed the fabric down out of his path and closed his hands caressingly round the firm globes, teasing the stiffly prominent nipples between his fingers. A startled gasp escaped from Bee. She looked down at those long fingers stroking the swollen pink peaks, flushed crimson and then shut her eyes tight again, her legs trembling beneath her. She should push him away, she should push him away, tell him to stop, *insist* that he stop.

Sergios swept her up off her feet while she was still struggling to reclaim her poise and strode into the bedroom to lay her down on the big wide bed. He hit a button above the headboard and she heard the door lock and she sat up, wrenching the towel back up over her exposed flesh.

'You're not going anywhere…' Sergios husked with raw masculine assurance, coming down to the bed on his knees and reaching for her.

'This is not a good idea,' Bee protested in a voice that without the slightest warning emerged as downright squeaky.

'You sound like a frightened virgin!' Sergios quipped, using one hand to tip up her chin and kiss her with hard, hungry fervour, his teeth nipping at her full lower lip, his tongue plunging in an erotic raid on her tender mouth. With his other hand he stroked the straining sensitive buds on her breasts and it was as if he had jerked a leash to pull her in, for instead of pushing back from him she discovered that she only wanted to go one way and that was closer.

'Sergios…' she cried against the demanding onslaught of his sensual mouth.

'*Filise me*…kiss me,' he urged, his strong hands roaming. 'I love your breasts.'

As sweet tempting sensation executed its sway over her treacherous body, Bee felt her lack of fight travelling through her like a debilitating disease. In a sudden move of desperation she flung herself sideways off the bed. She fell with a crash that bruised her hip and jolted every bone in her body and Sergios sat up to regard her with a look of bewilderment. He reached down to help her up again. 'How did you do that?' he questioned. 'Are you hurt?'

'No, but I had to stop what we were doing,' Bee volunteered jerkily, hauling at the towel again and feeling remarkably foolish.

'Why?' Sergios countered in frank astonishment.

Bee veiled her eyes and shut her mouth like a steel trap. 'Because I don't want to have sex with you.'

'That's a lie.' Smouldering eyes came to a screeching halt on her. 'I can tell when a woman wants me.'

Sitting on the wooden floor on a rug that did not make the floor any more comfortable, Bee marvelled that she did not simply scream and launch herself at him like a Valkyrie. He was like a dog with a bone; he wasn't going to give it up without a fight. 'I forgot myself for a moment…a weak moment. It won't happen again. You said you didn't want intimacy—'

'I've changed my mind,' Sergios admitted without skipping a beat.

Bee very nearly did scream then in frustration. 'But I haven't—changed my mind, that is.'

An utterly unexpected grin slanted his beautiful shapely mouth, lending a dazzling charisma to his already handsome features that no woman could have remained impervious to. He lounged fluidly back on the bed and shifted a graceful hand. 'So, then we deal, *yineka mou*—'

'*Deal?*' Bee parroted in a tone of disbelief.

'You're so uptight, Beatriz. You need a man like me to loosen you up.'

Tousled chestnut hair tumbling round her wildly flushed oval face, Bee stood up still clutching the towel. 'I don't want to loosen up. I'm quite happy as I am.'

Sergios released his breath in an impatient hiss. 'You can get pregnant if you want,' he proffered with a wry roll of his stunning dark eyes as if he were inviting her to take two pints of his blood. 'We're already saddled with three kids—how much difference could another one make?'

Her eyes wide with consternation at that shockingly unemotional appraisal, Bee backed away several feet. 'I think you're crazy.'

Sergios shook his arrogant dark head. 'Think outside the box, Beatriz. I'm trying to make a deal with you. As you're not in business, I'll explain—I give you what you want so that you give me what I want. It's that simple.'

'Except when it's my body on the table,' Bee replied in a tone of gentle irony. 'My body is not going to figure as any part of a deal with you or anybody else. We agreed that there would be no sex and I want to stick to that.'

'That is not the message your body is giving me, *latria mou*,' Sergios drawled softly.

'You're reading the signals wrong—maybe it's your healthy ego misleading you,' Bee suggested thinly as she hit the button he had used to lock the door to unlock it again.

As Bee leant across him Sergios hooked his fingers into the edge of the towel above her breasts. Immobilised, she looked up at him and collided with his dazzling eyes enhanced by ridiculously long lush lashes. Her heart seemed to jump into her throat.

'It's *not* my ego that's talking,' Sergios purred like a prowling big cat of the jungle variety.

'Yes, it is. Even though you don't really want me and I'm not your type.'

'I don't go for a particular type.'

'Zara? Your first wife? Let me remind you—*slim, glamorous*?' Bee stabbed without hesitation, watching his face tauten and pale as though she had struck him. The hand threatening the closure of the towel fell back and Bee was quick to take advantage of his uncharacteristic retreat. 'That's your type. I'm not and never could be.'

Sergios dealt her a steely-eyed appraisal. 'You don't know what turns me on'

'Don't I? Something you've been told you can't have. A challenge—that's all it takes to turn you on!' Bee hissed at him, fighting to hide the depth of her outrage. 'And I accidentally made myself seem like a challenge this evening. You're so perverse. If I was throwing myself at you, you would hate it.'

'Not right at this moment, I wouldn't,' Sergios purred in silken contradiction, running a hand down over the extended stretch of one long powerful thigh and by doing so drawing her attention to the tented effect of his tailored trousers over his groin. 'As you can see, I'm not in any condition to say no to a reasonable offer.'

As he directed her gaze to the evidence of his arousal Bee could feel a tide of mortified heat rush up from her throat to her hairline and she did not know where to look even as a kernel of secret heat curled in her pelvis. 'You're disgusting,' she said curtly and knew even as she said it that she didn't mean it. The knowledge that lust for her had put him in that state was strangely stimulating and there was something even more satisfying in that unsought but graphic affirmation of her femininity.

'Over dinner, think about what you want most,' Sergios advised lazily. 'And remember that there's nothing I can't give you.'

Consternation in her eyes, Bee stepped back from the bed, her oval face stiff with angry condemnation. 'Are you offering me money to sleep with you?'

Sergios winced. 'You're so literal, so blunt—'

'You just can't accept the word no, can you?' Bee launched at him in a furious flood. 'You even sank low enough to try and use a baby as a bargaining chip!'

'Of course you want a baby—I've watched you with my cousin's kids. Nobody could be that way with them if they didn't want one of their own,' Sergios opined with assurance. 'I've had enough experience with women to know that at some point in our marriage you will decide that you want a child of your own.'

'Right at this very moment,' Bee told him shakily, 'I'm wondering how I can possibly stay married to such a conniving and unscrupulous man!'

'Your mother, the kids, the fact that you don't like to fail at anything? You're not a quitter, Beatriz. I admire that in a woman.' Straightening his tie and finger-combing his black hair back off his brow, Sergios sprang off the bed, his big powerful body suddenly towering over her. 'But I do have one small word of warning for you,' he murmured in a tone as cool as ice. 'I don't talk about my first wife, Krista...*ever*, so leave her out of our...discussions.'

Shell-shocked from that spirited encounter and that final chilling warning, Bee got back into her cooling bath and sat there blinking in a daze. When he had touched her, a tide of such longing had gripped her that she had almost surrendered. But she wasn't stupid, and even though she had never been so strongly affected before by a man she had always accepted that sex and the cravings it awakened could be very powerful and seductive. Why else did the lure of sex persuade so many people to succumb to temptation and get into trouble over it? It might be a sobering discovery but she had only learned that she was as weak as any other human being.

After Krista's death—she who must not be mentioned—Sergios had become a notorious playboy. He had to be a very experienced lover and he knew exactly how to pull her strings and extract ladies who ought to have known better from towels, she allowed in growing chagrin. Well, he hadn't got the towel the whole way off, she told herself soothingly. With a male as ferociously determined and untamed as Sergios even the smallest victory ought to be celebrated.

It was silly how it actually hurt her pride that Sergios didn't *really* desire her. He was annoyed that his grandfather's presence in his home would force them to live a lie to conceal the reality that their marriage was a fake. His ego was challenged by the prospect of having to share a bed with a woman he had agreed not to touch, so he was trying to tear up the terms of their agreement by whatever means were within his power. Even so, she reckoned it had to be a very rare event for a man to try to seduce a woman by offering to get her pregnant.

Sergios could certainly think on his feet. Indeed he was utterly shameless and callous in pursuit of anything he wanted. But he was also, Bee thought painfully, extremely clever and far too shrewd for comfort. He had sensed the softy hiding below her practical surface and made an educated guess that the prospect of having her own child would have more pulling power with her than the offer of money or diamonds. And he had guessed right, *so* right in fact that she wanted to scream in frustration and embarrassment.

How could he see inside her heart like that? How could he have worked out already what she had only recently learned about herself? Only since she had been in daily contact with Paris, Milo and Eleni had Bee appreciated just how much she enjoyed being a mother. Out on a shopping trip she had bought baby clothes for Eleni and found herself drawn to examining the even tinier garments and the prams, newly afflicted by a broodiness that she had heard friends discuss but until then had never experienced on her own behalf.

But common sense warned her that right now she had

to stand her ground with Sergios. If she allowed him to walk over her so early in their marriage she would be the equivalent of a cipher within a few years, enslaved by her master's voice. He had to respect the boundaries they had set together. After all, he had Melita and other women in his life and she had no wish to join that specific party. The reflection tightened her muscles and made her head begin to ache as she appreciated that she truly was caught between a rock and a hard place with a man who attracted her but whom she could not have. She stretched back against the padded headrest, desperate to shed her tension and troubled thoughts. Sergios was an absolute menace to her peace of mind. He kept on moving the goalposts to suit himself. He was like a pirate on the high seas, always in pursuit of an advantage or a profit. But when it came to fencing with Bee he was just as likely to run aground on the rocks hidden beneath her deceptively calm surface.

When Sergios strolled into the bedroom, Bee was putting the finishing touches to her appearance. Her full-length blue evening dress fitted her like a glove without showing a surplus inch of flesh. His brilliant eyes narrowing, she watched in the mirror as Sergios subjected her to a considering appraisal.

'Sexy,' he pronounced approvingly.

Bee stiffened defensively. 'It's high at the neck and it doesn't even show my legs,' she argued.

Her immediate protest at his comment made amusement curl the corners of his handsome mouth. He scanned the lush swell of breast and derriere so clearly defined by the clinging fabric and said nothing at all.

No skin might be on show but the dress hugged her every curve and those she had in abundance.

He touched the end of a straying strand of her dark hair where it lay on her shoulder. 'Grow your hair again. I liked it longer.'

'Are you used to women doing what *you* like with their appearance?' Bee prompted a tad sourly.

'Yes,' Sergios proclaimed without a shred of discomfiture.

'Any other orders, boss?' Bee could not resist the crack.

'Smile and relax,' he urged. 'Nectarios is already very taken with you. He sees a big improvement in his great-grandsons—'

'My goodness, it's not down to my influence. I've only been with the children a few weeks—'

'But they didn't see that much of their own mother, so your attention means a great deal to them.'

'Why didn't they see much of their mother?'

'She was a popular TV presenter and rarely at home. Timon adored her.'

Suddenly she wanted to know if Sergios had adored Krista but she found that she couldn't imagine him in thrall to a woman, eager to impress and please. There was a bone-deep toughness and a reserve to Sergios that suggested that nothing less than pole position in a relationship would satisfy him. Yet he had only been twenty-one when he wed Krista and to marry so young he must have been a good deal less cynical about the institution of marriage. Comparing that to his attitude at their wedding the day before, Bee could only assume that he had got badly burned by Krista in some way. Of course there was the alternative view that losing Krista and their unborn child had hurt him so much that he had resolved never to fall in love or marry again.

Suddenly irritated by her curiosity, she asked herself why she should care. He had married her purely for the sake of Timon's children and she needed to remember that. This afternoon he had wanted to bed her and the motivation for that staggering turnaround was not that hard to work out, Bee reflected ruefully. How many other sexual options could this little Greek island offer Sergios? He was supposed to be on his honeymoon and if he wanted his grandfather to believe that it was a normal marriage he could scarcely ditch his bride and rush off to seek satisfaction in some other woman's bed. So, for the present, Sergios was trapped in a masquerade and Bee had become miraculously desirable through a complete absence of competition. Right now she was the only option her sensual Greek husband had. It was an acknowledgement that would certainly ensure she didn't develop a swollen head about the precise nature of her attractions.

Dinner was served on a terrace outside the formal dining room. The sun was going down over the sea in fiery splendour and the food was delicious. Bee ate with relish while Nectarios entertained her with stories about the history of the island and family ownership. As the two men finally succumbed to catching up on business, it amused her to recognise how alike Sergios and his grandfather were in looks and mannerisms and she told them she would not be offended if they switched to talking in Greek. She would have to learn the language and quickly, she recognised, grateful that learning languages came relatively easily to her, for it was essential that she be able to communicate effectively with the staff and the children. She did not want to be shut out of half of the conversations going on around her.

She contemplated Sergios over her fresh fruit dessert. The low lights gleamed over his cropped black hair and cast shadows on his strong bronzed profile. He was extraordinarily handsome and even the way he moved was sensual, she thought abstractedly, her eyes following the elegant arc inscribed by an eloquent hand as he spoke. When she glanced up and realised that Nectarios was watching her watch Sergios she went pink. A few minutes later she said it was time she looked in on the children and she left the table.

Having checked on the kids and agreed to take Paris down to the beach in the morning, Bee walked past the door of the main bedroom and on up the final flight of stairs to the bedroom at the top of the tower. Earlier that evening she had found the room and had decided that it would do her nicely as a bolthole. Hadn't she read somewhere recently that it was fashionable for couples with sufficient space in their homes to pursue a better night's sleep by occupying different bedrooms? Separate beds need not mean that anyone's relationship was on the rocks and that was what she would tell Sergios if he tried to object.

She slid on a light cotton nightdress that was far from glamorous, for she had disdained the silk and satin lingerie the personal shopper had directed her towards in London. She climbed into her big comfortable bed and lay with her cooling limbs splayed in a starfish shape to let all her tension drain away. In time this house and the new life she was leading would feel familiar and comfortable, she told herself soothingly.

The door opened and she jerked in surprise, lifting her head several inches off the pillow to peer across the room. The light from the stairwell fell on Sergios's lean strong features and glimmered over his bare, hair-roughened chest and the towel that appeared to be all he was wearing. Bee's short-lived relaxation dive-bombed and her limbs scissored back together again as she sat up and switched on the light.

'What are you doing in here?'

'As you've deserted the marital bed so must I. Wherever we sleep, we stay together,' Sergios spelt out with hard dark eyes and an unyielding angle to his jaw line.

Bee was intimidated by the amount of naked masculine flesh on view. He was tall and broad and, stripped, his big strong shoulders, powerful torso and tight flat stomach were distinctly imposing. 'Don't you dare take off that towel!' she warned him thinly.

'Don't be such a prude,' Sergios told her impatiently. 'I sleep naked. I always have.'

'I can't treat you like a brother if I've seen you naked!' Bee snapped back in embarrassment.

Sergios, engaged in wondering why she would want to treat him like a brother when his own intentions had roamed so far from the platonic plane, threw up both hands in a sudden gesture of exasperation. 'You must've seen loads of guys naked!'

'Oh, is that a fact?' Bee hissed, insulted by that assumption. 'You think I've slept with a lot of men?'

'I've had quite a few women. I'm not a hypocrite,' Sergios said drily.

Bee was seething. 'FYI some of us are a little more particular.'

'Did they all wear pyjamas?' Sergios asked, unable to resist that crack as his wondering gaze took in the full horror of the nightdress she wore: a baggy cotton monstrosity edged with fussy lace.

Bee cringed inwardly. 'There hasn't actually been anyone yet,' she admitted, hoping dismay at her inexperience would persuade him that she really did need her privacy.

Sergios came to an abrupt halt about ten feet from the foot of the bed. A frown had drawn his brows together. 'You can't mean that you've never had a lover…'

Bee reddened but she lifted and dropped both shoulders in a dismissive shrug as though the subject did not bother her at all. 'I haven't.'

Momentarily, Sergios was transfixed by the concept. He had believed virgins had died out around the same time as efficient contraception was developed. He had certainly never expected to find one in his bed. He swung on his heel and strode back out of the room without another word. Released from stasis, Bee breathed in slow and deep and switched out the light. Well, that news had certainly cooled his jets, she conceded. She had fallen out of the challenge category into the sort of unknown territory he evidently had no desire to explore.

But in that conviction Bee was wrong for the bedroom door opened again, startling her, and she raised herself on her elbows with a frown. Sergios was back, minus the towel and clad in a pair of black boxers, which did spectacularly little to conceal the muscular strength and bronzed beauty of his powerfully masculine body.

Sergios got into the far side of the bed in silence. A *virgin*, he was thinking with unholy fascination, a novelty calculated to appeal to even the most jaded palate.

Bee's toes encountered a masculine leg and she pulled hurriedly away as if she had been burned by the contact. His persistence in doing exactly what he wanted to do, regardless of her objections, was beginning to wear down even her nerves of steel.

'I've never gone to bed with a virgin before...' Sergios informed her in his deep drawl. 'In today's world you're as rare as a dinosaur.'

And at that astonishing assurance a bubble of unquenchable mirth formed and swelled in Bee's chest and then floated up into her throat to almost choke her before she finally gave vent to her laughter.

Sergios snaked out an arm and hauled her close. 'I wasn't trying to be funny.'

'Try to picture yourself as a d-dinosaur!' Bee advised, shaking with a hilarity she could not restrain. 'I just hope you weren't thinking of a T-Rex.'

Her laughter was even more of a surprise to a man who took life very seriously and sex more seriously still. He held her while wave after wave of uncontrollable amusement rippled through her curvy body and rendered her helpless. Her breasts rubbed his chest, her thighs shifted against his and he breathed in the soapy scent of her, picturing her equally helpless from passion in his arms. Desire roared through him afresh with a savagery that took even him aback.

Knotting one hand into the fall of her hair to hold her steady, Sergios dipped his tongue between her parted lips with erotic heat. All lingering amusement left her in the space of a moment as he plundered her ready response, nibbling and suckling at her full lower lip, skating an exploration over the sensitive roof of her mouth until her toes were curling and she was stretching up to him helpless in the grip of her need for more.

'Sergios…' she framed in vague protest when he let her breathe again.

'You'll still be a virgin in the morning,' Sergios murmured. 'I promise, *yineka mou.*'

CHAPTER SEVEN

BEE was trembling, insanely conscious of every erogenous zone on her body, but that saying that curiosity had killed the cat was playing in the back of her mind as well. Sergios was playing a game with her and she didn't know the rules, was convinced that she would live to regret letting down her defences. But there was a tightening sense of pressure at the heart of her that pulled tighter with every insidious flick of his tongue against hers and she could not resist its sway.

He inched the nightdress down over her slim shoulders, trapping her arms at the same time as he exposed her generous breasts. In the moonlight pouring through the filmy drapes those high round swells were the most tempting he had ever seen. He kneaded them with firm hands, closed his mouth hungrily to a rigid pink nipple and teased with his lips and his teeth while her back arched and she whimpered beneath his attentions. He switched his focus to her other breast, treating her to one tantalising caress after another, steadily utilising more pressure and urgency on her increasingly sensitised flesh.

It was like being taken apart and put together again

in a different sequence, Bee acknowledged in an agony of uncertainty that did nothing to stop the raging hunger that controlled her. She might never be the same again yet she still could not summon the will power to pull back or insist that he stop touching her. Her clenching fingers delved into his luxuriant hair while he stroked deliciously at her pointed nipples and kissed and licked his passage across the creamy slopes of her breasts before possessing her mouth again, drinking deep from her. She was wildly, seethingly aware of the brimming heat and moisture between her thighs and the ache of longing that had her hips digging into the bed beneath her. Her hands shifted back and forth across his satin-smooth shoulders as the knot of tension at the heart of her built and built. She pushed up to him desperate for more powerful sensation and she couldn't stay still then, couldn't find her voice, couldn't stop the gasps emanating from her throat either. And then suddenly it was all coalescing into one explosive response and she was arching and jerking and crying out in ecstasy as her body took her soaring onto another plane and there was nothing she could do to control any of it.

Afterwards, Bee wanted to leap out of the bed and run but there was nowhere to run to. The thought of cowering behind the bathroom door was not appealing. Still in his arms, she lay like a stone that had been dropped from a height, insanely conscious of her ragged breathing and racing heartbeat, not to mention the feel of his potent arousal against her hip. Dear heaven, what had she done?

'That was interesting,' Sergios purred with dark amusement. 'Definitely an ice breaker.'

'Er...you...?' Bee mumbled unevenly, conscious that events had been distinctly one-sided.

'I'll have a cold shower,' Sergios said piously.

Her face burning, Bee was relieved by the get-out clause. She knew it was selfish to be relieved but she was out of her depth and feeling it. She hadn't known, hadn't even guessed that she could reach a climax that way and she was not pleased that he had put her on that path of sexual discovery.

'You're a very passionate woman, *moli mou*,' Sergios intoned as he vaulted out of bed. 'Obviously Townsend wasn't the right guy for you.'

Bee went rigid. 'What do you know about Jon?'

Sergios paused in the doorway of the bathroom and swung back. 'More than you were prepared to tell me,' he admitted unrepentantly. 'I had him checked out.'

'You did...what?' Bee was righting her nightdress and trying to get out of bed at one and the same time, the simultaneous actions resulting in a clumsy manoeuvre that only infuriated her more. 'Why on earth did you do that? I *told* you he was a friend of mine—'

'But he wasn't—he was your ex, which made the little get-together in the bar rather less innocent, *moli mou*,' Sergios intoned, studying her furious face with level dark eyes. 'But, as I see it, since you never slept with him he doesn't really count.'

'If you ever touch me again I'll scream.'

'No complaints on that score. I love the way you

scream in my arms,' Sergios traded with silky sardonic bite and shut the bathroom door.

Bee knotted her hands into furious fists and contemplated throwing something at that closed door. It would be childish and she was *not* childish. But she had let herself down a bucketful by succumbing to his sexual magnetism. A tide of irritation swept through her then. No wonder he had called her a prude. She might feel mortified but they had hardly done anything in terms of sex. She was taking it all far too seriously and it would be much cooler to behave as though nothing worthy of note had happened.

But, without a doubt, Sergios was lethal between the sheets. The minute he got in she should have got out because compared with him she was a total novice and certain to come off worse from any encounter. And why had he checked Jon Townsend out after her single trivial meeting with her former boyfriend? Didn't Sergios trust anybody? Obviously not. How often had he been betrayed to become that suspicious of other human beings? It was a sobering thought and, although he had not been in love with her sister, Zara had agreed to marry him and then let him down. Perhaps had Bee chosen to be more honest with him he might had had more faith in her.

Around that point of self-examination, Bee must have drifted off to sleep because she wakened when Sergios stowed her into a cold bed. 'Er….what… where…*Sergios*?'

'Go back to sleep, Beatriz,' he intoned.

Her eyes fluttered briefly open on a view of the circular main bedroom in the moonlight and she simply turned over and closed her eyes again, too exhausted to protest. She woke alone in the morning, only the indent on the pillow across from hers telling her that she had had company. After a quick shower she put on Bermuda shorts and a sapphire-blue tee for the trip to the beach she had promised the boys. Nectarios was reading a newspaper out on the terrace where Androula brought Beatriz tea and toast.

'Sergios is in the office working,' his grandfather told her helpfully, folding his paper and setting it aside. 'What are you planning to do today?'

'Take the boys to the beach,' Bee confided.

'Beatriz…this is your honeymoon,' the elderly Greek remarked thoughtfully. 'Let the children take a back seat for a while and drag my grandson out of his office.'

Her imagination baulked at the image of getting Sergios to do anything against his will, but she could see that Nectarios was already picking up flaws in their behaviour as a newly married couple. He asked her about her mother and said he was looking forward to meeting her. Having eaten, Bee went off to find Sergios, although after their intimate encounter the night before she would have preferred to avoid him.

Sergios was working on a laptop in a sunlit room while simultaneously talking on the phone. Her troubled gaze locked to his bold bronzed profile. No matter how angry he made her she could never deny that he was drop-dead beautiful to look at any time of day. Finishing the call, he turned his sleek dark head, brilliant eyes welding to her, and her colour fluctuated wildly while her mouth ran dry at the impact of his gaze. 'Beatriz...'

'I'm taking the children to the beach. You should come with us. Nectarios is surprised that you've already gone back to work.'

'I don't do kids and beaches,' Sergios replied with a suggestive wince at the prospect of such a family outing.

Bee threw back her slim shoulders and spoke her mind, 'Then it's time you learned. Those kids need you...they *need* a father as well as a mother.'

'I don't know how to be a father. I never had one of my own—'

'That doesn't mean you can't do better for your cousin's children,' Bee cut in, immediately dismissing his argument in a manner that made his stubborn jaw line clench. 'Even an occasional father is better than no father at all. My father wasn't interested in me and I've felt that lack all my life.'

Under attack for his views, Sergios had sprung upright. He shrugged a broad shoulder and raked an impatient hand through his hair. His wide sensual mouth had taken on a sardonic curve. 'Beatriz—'

'No, don't you dare try to shut me up because I'm saying things you don't want to hear!' Beatriz shot back at him in annoyance. 'Even if you can only bring yourself to give the kids an hour once a week it would be better than no time at all. One *hour*, Sergios, that's all I'm asking for and then you can forget about them again.'

Sergios studied her grimly. 'I've told you how I feel. I married you so that you could take care of them.'

'Was that our "deal"?' Bee queried in a tone of scorn. 'I was just wondering. As you've already changed the terms on my side of the fence, why do you have to be so inflexible when it comes to your own?'

Sergios raised a brow. 'If I come to the beach will you share a room without further argument?'

Bee sighed in frustration. 'Relationships don't work like deals.'

'Don't they? Are you saying that you don't believe in give and take?'

'Of course, I do but I don't want to give or take sex like it's some sort of service or currency,' Bee told him with vehement distaste.

'Sex and money make the world go round,' Sergios jibed.

'I'm better than that—I'm worth more than that and so should you be. We're not animals or sex workers.'

Her love of frankness was peppered with an unexpected penchant for drama that amused him and he marvelled that he could ever have considered her plain or willing to please. With those vivid green eyes, that perfect skin and ripe pink mouth she was the very striking image of natural beauty. He could still barely believe that she was the only woman he had ever met to have refused him. While rejection might gall him her unattainability was a huge turn-on for him as well and when she had admitted she was a virgin he had understood her reluctance a great deal better and valued her all the more.

Recognising the tension in the atmosphere, Bee stiffened. He gave a look, just a look from his smouldering dark golden eyes and her nipples tightened, her tummy flipped and moist heat surged between her thighs. Colouring, she hastily fixed her eyes elsewhere, outraged that she could have so little control over her own body.

'All right,' she said abruptly, spinning back to deal him a withering look that almost made him laugh. 'If you do the hour a week with the children without complaining, I won't argue about sharing a room any more. Over breakfast I realised that your grandfather doesn't miss a trick and he is suspicious.'

'I said a long time ago that I would never marry again and he knows me well. Naturally he's sceptical about our marriage.'

'See you down at the beach,' Bee responded a touch sourly, for she was not pleased that she had had to give way on the bedroom issue. Unfortunately her previous attempts to persuade Sergio to get involved with his cousin's children had proved fruitless and if there was anything she could do to improve that situation she felt she had to make the most of the opportunity.

Karen was on duty and the children were already dressed in their swimming togs while a beach bag packed with toys and drinks awaited her. Paris led the way down through the shady belt of pine forest to the crisp white sand. They were peering into a rock pool when Sergios arrived. Wearing denim cut-offs with an unbuttoned shirt and displaying a flat and corrugated muscular six-pack that took Bee's breath away, Sergios strode across the sand to join them. The boys made a beeline for him, touchingly eager for his attention. Paris chattered about boy things like dead crabs, sharks and fishing while Bee held Milo and Eleni's hands to prevent them from crowding Sergios. She paddled with the toddlers in the whispering surf to amuse them. When Paris began building a sandcastle, Milo and Eleni ran back to join their brother.

Sergios walked across to Bee.

'Thirty-two minutes and counting,' she warned him in case he was thinking of cutting his agreed hour short.

An appreciative grin slashed his handsome mouth. 'I haven't got a stopwatch on the time.'

'What happened to your father?' she asked in a rush before she could lose her nerve.

As he looked out to sea his eyes narrowed. 'He died at the age of twenty-two trying to qualify as a racing driver.'

'You never knew him?'

'No, but even if Petros had lived he wouldn't have taken anything to do with me.' Sergios volunteered that opinion with telling derision. 'My mother, Ariana, was a teenage receptionist he knocked up on one of the rare days that he showed up to work for Nectarios.'

'Did your mother ever tell him about you?' Bee prompted.

'He refused her calls and got her sacked when she tried to see him. She didn't know she had any rights and she had no family to back her up. Petros had no interest in being a father.'

'It must have been very tough for so young a girl to get by as a single parent.'

'She developed diabetes while she was pregnant. Her

health was never good after my birth. I stole to keep us,' he admitted succinctly. 'By the age of fourteen I was a veteran car thief.'

'From that to...*this*...' Her spread hands encompassed the big opulent house beyond the forest and the island owned by his grandfather. 'Must have been a huge step for you.'

'Nectarios was very patient. It must've been even harder for him. I was poorly educated, bitter about my mother's death and as feral as an animal when he first employed me. But he never gave up on me.'

'You were probably a more worthwhile investment of his time than the father you never met,' Bee offered.

Sergios surveyed her steadily, his stunning gaze reflecting the sunlight as he slowly shook his arrogant head in apparent wonderment at that view. 'Only you would think the best of me after what I've just told you about my juvenile crime record, *yineka mou*.'

Bee coloured, noticed that Milo was approaching the sea with a bucket and sped off to watch over the little boy. But it was Sergios who stepped from behind her and scooped up Milo as he teetered uncertainly ankle deep in the surging water, swinging the child up in the air so that he laughed uproariously before depositing him and, thanks to Bee's efforts, a filled bucket of water back beside the sandcastle.

Eleni her silent companion, Bee spread the rug and Sergios threw himself down beside her. As she knelt he closed a hand into her chestnut hair and lifted her head, searching her oval face with brooding eyes. She gazed back at him with a bemused frown. 'What do you want from me?' she questioned in frustration.

'Right now?' Sergios released a roughened laugh that danced along her taut spine like trailing fingertips. 'Anything you'll give me. Haven't you worked that out yet?'

He crushed her mouth under his, tasting her with an earthy eroticism that fired up every skin cell in her quivering body. Hunger rampaged through her like a fire burning out of control and the strength of that hunger scared her so much that she thrust him back from her, her attention shooting past him to check that the children were still all right. Paris had been watching them kiss and he turned away, embarrassed by the display but no more so than Bee was. Sergio rested back on an elbow, one raised thigh doing little to conceal the bold outline of his arousal below the denim. Suddenly as hot as though she were roasting in the fires of hell, Bee dragged her gaze from him and watched the children instead.

'You're trying to use me because I'm the only woman available to you right now,' she condemned half under her breath.

Sergios ran a fingertip down her arm and she turned her head reluctantly to collide with his glittering dark eyes. 'Do I really strike you as that desperate?'

Her full mouth compressed. 'I didn't say *desperate*.'

'I can leave the island any time I like to scratch an itch.'

'Not if you want to convince your grandfather that you're a happily married man.'

'I could easily manufacture a business crisis that demanded my presence,' Sergios countered lazily. 'You have a remarkably low opinion of your own attraction.'

'Merely a realistic one. Men have never beaten a path to my door,' Bee admitted without concern. 'Jon was special for a while but once he realised that my mother and I were a package he backed off.'

'And married a wealthy judge's daughter. He's ambitious, not a guy with a bleeding heart,' Sergios commented, letting her know how much he knew and making her body tense with resentment over the professional snooping that had delivered such facts. 'Doesn't it strike you as odd that he should now be approaching you as the representative of a children's charity?'

Bee ignored the hint that Jon was an opportunist because she did not intend to adopt Sergios's cynicism as her yardstick when it came to judging people's motives. 'No. As your wife I could be of real use to the charity.'

'And as my ex-wife you could be of even more use to Jon,' Sergios completed with sardonic bite. 'Be careful. You could be his passport to another world.'

'I'm not stupid.'

'Not stupid, but you are naive and trusting.' He studied her with amusement. 'After all, you ignored all the warnings and married me.'

'If you treat me with respect I will treat you the same,' Bee swore. 'I don't lie or cheat and I don't like being manipulated.'

Sergios laughed out loud. 'And I'm a very manipulative guy.'

'I know,' Bee said gravely. 'But now you've got me in the same bed that's as far as it goes.'

His curling black lashes semi-concealed his stunning eyes. 'That would be such a waste, Beatriz. We have the opportunity, the chemistry.'

'With all due respect, Sergios,' Beatriz murmured sweetly, cutting in, 'that's baloney. You only want to bed me because you believe it'll make us seem more intimate and therefore more of a couple for your grandfather's benefit. And while I think he's a lovely old man, I don't want to go that far to please.'

'I can make you want me,' Sergios reminded her smooth as silk but it was the tough guy talking, his dark eyes hard as ebony, his strong bone structure taut with controlled aggression.

'But only in the line of temporary insanity. It doesn't last,' Bee traded, longing for the smile and the laughter that had been there only minutes earlier and suddenly recognising another danger.

It would be so easy to fall for this man she had married, she grasped with a sudden stab of apprehension. He wasn't just gorgeous to look at, he was an intensely charismatic man. Unfortunately he had very few scruples. If she let him, he would use her and discard her again without thought or regret. Where would she be then? Hopelessly in love with a guy who didn't love her back and who betrayed her with other women? She suppressed a shudder at that daunting image, and her heart, which he had made beat a little faster, steadied again.

A ball suddenly thumped into her side and the breath

she was holding in escaped in a startled huff. Instantly Sergios was vaulting upright and telling Paris off, but Bee was relieved by the interruption and quick to intervene. She threw the ball back to the boys, retrieved Eleni from the shells she was collecting and joined in their game.

Unappreciative of the fact that she was using the children as a convenient shield, Sergios was equally challenged by the idea that she could so easily discard the idea of becoming a proper wife. He thought of the countless women who had gone to extraordinary lengths to get him to the altar and failed and then he looked at Beatriz, distinctly unimpressed by what he had to offer in bed or out of it. He was out of his element with a woman who put a value on things without a price. He didn't do feelings, fidelity or...virgins. Basically he operated on the belief that women were all the same, money greased the wheels of his affairs and he had few preferences. That ideology had carried him along a safe smooth path after his first marriage right up to the present day. But nothing in that credo fitted Beatriz Blake. In her own quiet way she was a total maverick.

A manservant came down to the beach to tell Sergios about an important call. He departed and Bee tried not to care that he had gone, leaving behind a space that absolutely nothing else could fill. It was impossible to be unaware of a personality and a temperament as larger than life as Sergios Demonides. When Bee trekked up from the beach late afternoon with two tired little boys and an equally tired and cross little girl, she was damp and sandy and pink from the sun in spite of her high factor sun cream.

Having fed Eleni and spent some time cuddling the little girl while chatting with the nannies about the child's upcoming surgery that would hopefully improve her hearing, Bee left the nursery and went for a shower before changing for dinner. In the bedroom she found several boxes of exclusive designer nightwear on the bed in her size, items fashioned to show off the female body for a man's benefit and not at all the sort of thing that Bee wore for comfort and cosiness. She could barely believe Sergios's nerve in ordering such items for her but it was certainly beginning to sink in on her that he was a very determined man. When she returned to the bedroom, clad in her own light robe, Sergios was there and she stiffened, unaccustomed to the lack of privacy entailed in sharing a bedroom. Engaged in tying the sash on the robe to prevent it from falling open, she hovered uncomfortably.

'Did you order those nightgowns for me?' she pressed.

'Yes. Why not?'

'They're not the sort of thing I would wear.'

Sergios shrugged off the assurance. 'My grandfather has decided to return to his home.'

'I thought it was uninhabitable.'

'Two rooms are but it's a substantial property. I think that was an excuse to allow him to check us out,' Sergios confided wryly. 'He's taking the children and their nannies back with him.'

Her head flew up, green eyes wide with surprise and

bewilderment 'Why on earth would he take the kids with him?'

'Because it's a rare newly married couple who want three children around on their honeymoon,' Sergios drawled, his face impassive. 'Don't make a fuss about this. It's a well-meant offer and he is their grandfather—'

'Yes, I know he is *but*—'

'Objecting isn't an option,' Sergios sliced in with sudden impatience. 'It's a done deal and it would look strange if we turned him down.'

Bee could not hide her consternation at the arrangement that had been agreed behind her back. He had married her to act as a mother to those children but it seemed that she was not entitled to the rights or feelings of a mother if they conflicted with his wishes. 'Yes, but the children are just getting used to me. It's unsettling for them to be passed around like that.'

'You can go over and see them every day if you like.' His beautiful wilful mouth took on a sardonic slant. 'First and foremost you are my wife, Beatriz. Start acting like one.'

Bee reddened as though she had been disciplined for wrongdoing, her temper flaring inside her. 'Is that an order, sir?'

'*Ne*…yes, it is,' Sergios confirmed without hesitation or any hint of amusement. 'Let's keep it simple. I tell you what I want, you do it.'

Those candid words still echoing in her ears, Bee vanished back into her bathroom to do her make-up. Being ordered around when she was naked below a wrap didn't feel right or comfortable. But then she never had liked being told what to do. In addition she was very angry with him. He had encouraged her to act like a mother, only to snatch the privilege back again when it no longer suited him. *Act like a wife?* If she did that he wouldn't like it at all…for a wife would make demands.

CHAPTER EIGHT

CLEARLY in no mood to make the effort required to convince the staff that he was an attentive new husband, Sergios did not join Bee at the dinner table until she was halfway through her meal and the silence while they ate together screamed in her ears like chalk scraping down a blackboard.

'I didn't think you'd be the type to sulk.'

'Am I allowed to shout at you, sir?'

'Enough already with the sir,' Sergios advised impatiently.

Her appetite dying, Bee pushed her plate away.

'I'll take you out sailing tomorrow morning,' he announced with the air of a man expecting a round of applause for his thoughtfulness.

'Lucky me,' Bee droned in a long-suffering voice.

'Later this week, I'll take you over to Corfu to shop.'

'I hate shopping—do we have to?'

The silence moved in again.

'When I married you I believed you were a reasonable, rational woman,' Sergios volunteered curtly over the dessert course.

'I believed you when you said you wanted a platonic

marriage,' Bee confided. 'Just goes to show how wrong you can be about someone.'

'Do you think your own mother will be fooled by the way we're behaving into believing that this is a happy marriage?'

Hit on her weakest flank by that question, Bee paled.

'Don't wait up for me,' Sergios told her as he too pushed away his plate, the food barely touched. 'Last month I took over my grandfather's seat on the island council and it meets tonight. I'll stay for a drink afterwards.'

Frustrated by his departure when nothing between them had been resolved, Bee phoned her mother and lied through her teeth about how very happy she was. She then tried very hard to settle down with a book but her nerves continued to zing about like jumping beans and at well after ten that evening she decided that, as she wasn't the slightest bit tired, vigorous exercise might at least dispel her tension. At her request a pole had been fitted in the house gym and she had politely ignored Sergios's mocking enquiry as to what she intended to do with it. Like all too many people Sergios evidently assumed that pole dancing was a lewd activity best reserved for exotic dancers in sleazy clubs. Clad in stretchy shorts and a crop top, Bee did her warm-up exercises to loosen up before putting on her music.

Sergios was resolutely counting his blessings as he drove back along the single-track road to his home. Unhappily a couple of drinks and all the jokes with his colleagues on the island council that had recognised his status as a newly married man hadn't taken the edge off his mood. In fact he was engaged in reminding himself that being married was by its very nature tough. Learning how to live with another person was difficult. Nobody knew that better than him, which was why he had cherished his freedom for so long. Indeed the lesson of having once lost his freedom was engraved on his soul in scorching letters, for Sergios never forgot or forgave his own mistakes. He knew he should be grateful that Beatriz was so very attached to children who were not her own. She was a good woman with a warm heart and strong moral values. He knew he should be appreciative of the fact that if he came home unexpectedly he was highly unlikely to walk into a wild party...

When he walked into the lounge, however, he was vaguely irritated to find that Beatriz had not waited up for him, thereby demonstrating her concern for his state of mind and their marriage. He was hugely taken aback to recognise that he actually *wanted* her to do wifely things of that nature. That she had just taken herself off to bed was definitely not a compliment. It was hardly surprising, he acknowledged in sudden exasperation, that Beatriz should be confused about what he wanted from her when he no longer knew himself.

The bedroom, though, was also empty and Androula, plump and disapproving in her dressing gown, answered his call and informed him that Beatriz was in the gym. Having dispensed with his tie and his jacket, Sergios followed the sound of the music but what he saw when he glanced through the glass doors of the gymnasium brought him to a sudden stunned halt.

Beatriz was hanging upside down on a pole. By the

time he got through the door she was doing a hand-stand and swirling round the pole, legs splaying in a distinctly graphic movement that he would not have liked her to do in public. He was astonished by how fit she was as she went through an acrobatic series of moves. That stirring display was so unexpected from such a quiet conservative woman that it made it seem all the more exciting and illicit. He watched her kick, toes pointed, slender muscles flexing in a shapely leg and in a rounded, deliciously plump derriere. Around that point he decided simply to enjoy the show. As she undulated sexily against the pole, full breasts thrust out, hips shifting as though on wires, he was hard as a rock and her sinuous roll on the floor at the foot of the pole was frankly overkill.

'Beatriz?' Sergios husked.

In consternation at the sound of his voice, Bee flipped straight back upright, wondering anxiously for how long she had had an audience. Brilliant dark eyes welded to her, Sergios was by the door, tall, darkly handsome and overwhelmingly masculine. Lifting her towel to dry the perspiration from her face, she paused only to switch off the music.

'When did you get back?'

'Ten minutes ago. How long have you been doing that for?'

'About three years,' she answered a little breathlessly, drawing level with him. 'It was more fun than the other exercise classes.'

His gaze smouldering, he bent his dark head and crushed her parted lips hotly beneath his, ravishing her mouth with the staggering impact of a long, drugging kiss. A shiver of sensual shock ran through her as his arms came round her and she felt the hard urgency of his erection against her stomach.

'*Se thelo*...I want you,' he breathed raggedly. 'Let's make this a real marriage.'

Taken aback by that proposition, Bee tried to step back but Sergios had a strong arm braced to her spine as he walked her down the corridor. 'We need to think about this,' she reasoned, struggling to emerge from that potent kiss, which had made her head swim.

'No, I believe in gut instinct. We've been thinking far too much about things,' Sergios fired back with strong masculine conviction. 'You're not supposed to agonise over everything you do in life and look for all the pitfalls, Beatriz. Some things just happen naturally.'

He thrust open their bedroom door, whirled her round and devoured her mouth hungrily beneath his again, his tongue darting into the tender interior of her mouth, setting up a chain reaction of high voltage response inside her. This, she registered, was the sort of thing he believed should happen naturally, but from Bee's point of view there was nothing natural about the fact that she was trembling and unable to think straight. The force of his passion knocked her off balance while a raging fire leapt up inside her to answer it. Locked together, they stumbled across the room and down on the bed, his hands smoothing over her Lycra-clad curves with an appreciative sound deep in his throat.

'I don't want anyone else seeing you dance like that,' Sergios spelt out. 'It's too sexy—'

'But that's how I keep fit—it's only exercise.'

'It's incredibly erotic,' Sergios contradicted, wrenching off the shorts with impatient hands.

'We really ought to be discussing this,' she told him anxiously.

A heart-breaking smile slashed his beautiful mouth. 'I don't want to talk about it…we've talked it to death.'

That smile made her stretch up to kiss him again, her fingertips smoothing over a hard cheekbone and delving into his silky black hair with a licence she had never allowed herself before. If they made love he would be hers as no other man had ever been and she wanted that with every fibre of her being and a strength of longing she had not known she was capable of feeling. Unbuttoning his shirt, she pulled it off his shoulders and he cast it off, laughing at her impatience. Standing up, he dispensed with the rest of his clothing at efficient speed and a tingling hum of arousal thrummed through her as she looked at his powerfully aroused body. He was ready for her.

Sergios pulled her up and peeled her free of the crop top and the sports bra she wore beneath. With a groan of sensual satisfaction he cupped the creamy swell of her breasts and licked and stroked the swollen pink tips until she shivered. 'Perfect,' he husked.

Liquid heat pooled between her legs as he located the damp stretch of fabric between her legs and eased a finger beneath it to trace her delicate centre. She twisted beneath his touch and lifted her hips as he took off her knickers. He kissed a trail down over her writhing length until he found the most truly sensitive spot of all. As he lingered there to subject her to the erotic torment of his skilled mouth and hand, she had to fight her innate shyness with all her might.

Had she been in control it would have been wrenched from her by the power of her response. As it was, she was free to abandon herself to sensation and she did, her head moving restively back and forth on the pillow, shallow gasps escaping her throat as her hips rose and fell on the bed. She was at the very height of excitement before he came over her and entered her in one effortless stroke. Even so there was still a stark moment of pain and she cried out as he completed his possession, driving home to the very core of her. The discomfort swiftly ebbed even as his invasive hard male heat awakened and stimulated her need again.

'Sorry,' he sighed with intense male pleasure. 'I was as gentle as I could be.'

'You're forgiven,' she murmured, very much preoccupied as she arched her spine and lifted her hips to accept more of him, desire driving her to obey her own needs.

'You're so tight,' he breathed with earthy satisfaction, rising up on his elbows and withdrawing only to thrust back deeper into her receptive body in a movement that was almost unbearably exhilarating.

Her breath catching in her throat, her heart thundering with growing fervour she shut her eyes, revelling in the feel of him inside her. She writhed beneath him as he drove deeper with every compelling thrust and his fluid rhythm increased, plunging her into an intoxicating world of erotic and timeless delight. The excitement took over until all she was aware of was him and the hot, sweet pleasure gathering stormily at the heart of her. She reached an explosive climax and plunged over the edge into ecstasy, gasping and writhing in voluptuous abandon.

Shuddering over her, Sergios cried out with uninhibited fulfilment gripped by the longest, hottest climax of his life. As her arms came round him to hold him he pulled back, however, releasing her from his weight. He threw himself back against the pillows next to her, enforcing a separation she was not prepared for at that most intimate of moments.

'That was unbelievably good, *yineka mou*,' Sergios savoured, breathing in a lungful of much-needed air. 'Thank you.'

Thank you? Bee blinked in bewilderment at that polite salutation and reached for his hand, closing her fingers round his and turning over to snuggle into his big powerful body, spreading her fingers across a stretch of his warm muscular torso. He stiffened at the contact.

'I don't do the cuddling thing, *glikia mou*.'

'You're not too old to learn,' Bee told him dreamily, dazed by what they had just shared but also happy at the greater closeness she sensed between them. 'You just persuaded me to do something spontaneous and that's not usually my style.'

Recognising the truth that Beatriz almost always had a smart answer for everything, Sergios made no comment. Instead he settled curious dark golden eyes on her flushed face. 'I hurt you. Are you sore?'

Bee gave a little experimental shift of her hips and winced. 'A little.'

'Shame,' he pronounced with regret, a sensual curve to his firm mouth. 'Right now, I would love to do it all over again but I'll wait until tomorrow.'

'You didn't use a condom,' Bee remarked, her surprise at that oversight patent.

'I'm clean. I have regular health checks. Hopefully we'll get away with it this once on the contraception front. I don't keep condoms here,' he admitted bluntly. 'I don't bring women to my home. I never have done.'

There were so many questions brimming on her lips but she wouldn't let herself ask them. She liked the fact that the room and bed had not been used by other women. But she did want to know about his first wife—there was not even a photo of Krista on display in the house. Then there was his mistress, and where Bee and Sergios were to go from here, but that thorny question would be a case of too much too soon for a guy who had fought so hard to retain his freedom and keep his secrets. He wasn't going to change overnight, she told herself ruefully.

Let's make this a real marriage, he had said in the gym. Had he truly meant it? Or had a desire for sex momentarily clouded his judgement when her dancing awakened his libido? Could he simply have told her what he thought she wanted to hear? Uneasy at that suspicion, Bee tensed but refused to lower herself to the level of asking him if he was genuinely committed to their marriage. Expressing doubt, after all, might just as easily encourage what she most feared to come about.

'We'll put a pole up in the bedroom so that you can exercise in here where nobody else can see you,' Sergios informed her lazily.

Bee could not believe her ears. His persistence on that subject was a revelation. He had not been joking in the gym when he said he didn't want anyone else to see her dancing. 'I didn't think you would be such a prude.'

'You're my wife,' Sergios reminded her, but his face was taut, as if giving her that label pained him.

Looking up into those darkly handsome features, Bee could already see the wheels of intellect turning as he questioned their new intimacy. How did he really feel about that? She lowered her lashes, refusing to agonise over something she had no control over. Living with Sergios would be a roller-coaster ride and as he did not suffer anything in silence she had no doubt that she would soon know exactly how he felt.

'I'll be late back tonight,' Sergios told her, sinking down on the side of the bed. He hesitated for a split second before he grasped the hand that she had instinctively extended to stop him leaving the room.

Still half asleep, for it was very early, Bee studied him drowsily, noting the brooding tension etched into his face while loving the warmth of his hand in hers and the golden intensity of his gaze. 'Why?'

'It's the anniversary of Krista's death today. I usually attend a memorial service with her parents and dine with them afterwards,' Sergios explained, his intonation cool and unemotional.

Taken aback, for although they had been married for

six weeks he still never ever mentioned his first wife, Bee nodded and belatedly noticed the sombre black suit that he wore.

'It's an annual event,' he said with an uneasy shrug. 'Not something I look forward to.'

She bit back the comment that some people regarded a memorial service as an opportunity to celebrate the life of the departed. 'Would you like me to go with you?' she asked uncertainly.

'That's a generous offer but I don't think Krista's parents would appreciate it. She was their only child. I get the impression that they don't want to be reminded that my life has moved on,' Sergios commented, compressing his handsome mouth with the stubborn self-discipline that was so much a part of his character.

Her ignorance of what he was feeling troubled Bee for the rest of the day. But then she was madly, hopelessly in love with Sergios and prone to worrying about what was on his mind. Although the sexual chemistry they shared was indisputably fantastic, that wasn't what had awakened more tender feelings in her heart. It was while Bee was busily working out what made Sergios tick that she had fallen head over heels in love with him.

When he was away on business she felt as though she were only half alive. Deprived of his powerful and often unsettling charismatic presence, she would watch her phone like a lovesick adolescent desperate for his call, count the hours until he came home and then lavish attention on him in bed until he purred like a big jungle cat. He was in her heart as though he had always been there, strong and stubborn and infuriatingly unpredictable.

In learning to love him she had also recognised his vulnerabilities. He was unsure how to behave with the children because his mother's ill health had deprived him of a carefree childhood. Although Bee had come from a similar background the burden of caring had been lightened in her case by her mother's deep affection. Sergios's mother, however, had been very young and immature and might possibly have resented the adverse impact of a child on her life and health. For whatever reasons, Sergios had not received the love and support he had needed to thrive during his formative years.

Within days of being removed to their grandfather's home on the other side of the bay Paris, Milo and Eleni had made it clear how much they were missing Bee and Sergios had swiftly accepted the inevitable and agreed to their return. With Bee's support since then Sergios had gradually spent more time with his cousin's kids, getting to know them so that he no longer froze when Milo hurled himself at him or looked uneasily away when Eleni opened her arms to him. Bridges were being built. Paris turned to Sergios for advice, Milo brought his ball and Eleni smiled at him when he risked getting close. Sergios was slowly learning how to accept affection and how to respond to it.

Bee had been relieved when she received the proof that their unprotected lovemaking on the first night they had spent together had not led to her conceiving a child. In her opinion an unplanned pregnancy would have been a disaster for their marriage. Sergios was very much a man who needed to make the decision that he wanted to be a father for himself. Yet when she had told him that he need not worry on that score, he had shrugged.

'I wasn't worrying about that,' he had insisted. 'If you had conceived we would have coped.'

But Bee would not have been happy while he merely 'coped'. She only wanted to have a baby with a man who was actively *keen* for her to have his baby. She did not want Sergios to make the best of an accidental conception or to offer her the option of a pregnancy because she was broody: she wanted him to make a choice that he wanted a child with her, a child of his own.

The weeks they had shared on the island had not been only about the children. Bee had stopped fretting about the future and had lived for the moment and Sergios had made many of those moments surprisingly special. He had proudly given her a tour of the wheelchair-friendly cottage in the grounds where her mother was to live. A carer whom Emilia would choose for herself from a list that had already been drawn up would come in every day to help her cope. Bee could hardly wait to see the older woman's face when she enjoyed her first cup of tea on the sunny terrace with its beautiful view of the bay.

Sergios had also flown Bee to Corfu for a week. The busy streets lined with elegant Italianate buildings, sophisticated shops and art studios had delighted her and one afternoon when Sergios had briefly lost her in the crowds he had anchored his hand to hers and kept it there for the rest of the day. He had bought her a beautiful silver icon she admired and they had had drinks on The Liston, an arcaded building modelled on the Rue de Rivoli in Paris. By the time they had returned to their designer hotel she was giggly and tipsy and he had made passionate love to her until dawn when she fell asleep in his arms. Opening her eyes again on his handsome features in profile as he worked at his laptop, getting some work out of the way before the day began, she had seen into her own heart and had known in the magic of that moment that she loved him. Loved him the way she had never thought she would ever love any man, with tenderness and appreciation of both his flaws and his strengths.

They had enjoyed numerous trips out and about on Orestos. He had shown her all over the island, had taken her swimming and sailing and snorkelling, letting the children join in whenever possible. He had enjoyed the fact that she was energetic enough to share the more physical pursuits with him. She also now knew that he was very competitive when it came to building sandcastles or fishing and that he was crazy about ice cream. He also loved it when she and the children were there to greet him when he came home from a trip. There was an abyss of loneliness deep inside Sergios that she longed to assuage.

With such uneasy thoughts dominating her mind about Krista's memorial service and what those memories might mean to her husband, Bee could not settle that afternoon. She received another text from Jon Townsend, who had stayed in surprisingly regular contact with her since her arrival in Greece, and suppressed a sigh. Her ex-boyfriend had sent her reams of information about the charity he was involved with and was keen to set up a meeting with her during her approaching visit to the UK.

On such a beautiful day it had seemed a good idea to collect Milo from his playgroup in town on foot rather than drive there as she usually did. The summer heat, however, was intense and by the time she picked up Milo Bee was questioning the wisdom of having trudged all the way along the coast road, particularly when she had no alternative other than to walk back again. Milo, in comparison, hopped, jumped and skipped along by her side with the unvarnished energy that was his trademark.

She was walking through the town square with Eleni dozing below a parasol in her pushchair when Nectarios waved at them from a table outside the taverna. He wore his faded peaked cap, and only a local would have recognised him as the powerful business tycoon that he still was even in semi-retirement. She guessed by his clothing that he had been out sailing in the small yacht he kept at the harbour and she crossed to that side of the street.

'What are you doing here on foot?' he asked with a frown, spinning out a chair for her and snapping his fingers for the proprietor's attention.

'Milo was at his playgroup. It didn't seem quite so warm when I left the house.'

'My lift will be here in ten minutes. You can all ride back with me.' The old man ordered drinks for Bee and the children while calmly allowing Milo to clamber onto his lap and steal his cap to try it on and then treat it like a frisbee.

While they sat there enjoying the welcome shade of the plane tree beside the terrace various passers-by came over to chat to Nectarios. Bee was daily picking up more Greek words and she understood odd snatches of the conversations about fishing trips, weddings and christenings. Tomorrow she was returning to London, where Eleni would have surgery on her ears, and when they came back to the island her mother would be travelling with her. She was helping Eleni with her feeding cup when she became aware of a flutter of whispers around her. Glancing up, Bee noticed the statuesque blonde walking through the square. She wore a simple figure-hugging white dress and she had that swaying walk and brash confidence that men almost always seemed to find irresistible. Certainly every man in the vicinity was staring in admiration.

'Who's that?' she asked the man beside her, who had faltered into a sudden silence. 'Is she a tourist?'

The woman looked directly at them with big brown eyes and a sultry smile on her red-tinted lips, her attention lingering with perceptible curiosity on Bee.

Nectarios gave the blonde a faint nod of acknowledgement. 'That's Melita Thiarkis.'

That familiar first name struck Bee like a slap but she would have thought nothing of it if Nectarios had not looked distinctly ill at ease.

'And she's...who?' she pressed, hating herself for her persistence in the face of his discomfiture.

'A fashion designer in Athens, but she was born on the island and maintains a property here.'

That fast Bee's stomach threatened to heave and she struggled to control her nausea with perspiration beading her brow and her skin turning unpleasantly clammy. The blonde *had* to be Sergios's mistress, Melita. There could not be such a coincidence. Indeed Nectarios's embarrassment at her appearance had confirmed the fact. But Bee was in shock at the news that Melita was actually staying on the island. That possibility had not even occurred to her and she had naively assumed that Orestos offered Sergios no opportunity to stray. But how many evenings had he left her alone for several hours while he attended island council meetings? Or to visit his grandfather's home? Lately there had been several such occasions and she had thought nothing of them at the time. Had she been ridiculously naive?

'May I offer you some advice?' Nectarios enquired as the four-wheel drive that had picked them up raised a trail of dust on the winding, little-used road back to the big white house with the tower on the headland.

Bee shot him a glance from troubled eyes. 'Of course.'

'Don't put pressure on my grandson. Give him the time to recognise what you have together. His first marriage was very unhappy and it left deep scars.'

The old man was the product of another generation in which men and women were not equal and women expected and even excused male infidelity. Bee had no such guiding principle to fall back on and she could not excuse what she could not live with. And she knew that she would never be able to live in silence with the suspicion that Sergios might have laid lustful hands on another woman while he was sharing a bed with Bee.

Oh, how the mighty had fallen, Bee conceded wretchedly. Now she had to face up to the reality that she had allowed Sergios to run their marriage *his* way rather than hers. They had not renegotiated the terms of their original marriage plan. There had been no earnest discussions, no agreements and no promises made on either side. For almost two months they had coasted along without the rules and boundaries that she had feared might make Sergios feel trapped. Take things slowly, Bee had thought in her innocence, eager to pin her husband down, but too sensible not to foresee the probable risks of demanding too much from him upfront.

Now she was paying the price of not frankly telling him that he could not have her *and* a mistress. Strange how she had no doubt that he would angle for that option if he thought he could get away with it. Bee was well aware of how ruthless Sergios could be. In any confrontation he was hardwired to seek the best outcome that he could. Sometimes he manoeuvred people into doing what he wanted purely as a means of amusement. She had stood on the sidelines of his life watching him, learning how he operated and monitoring her own behaviour accordingly. Although she loved him she didn't tell him that and she certainly didn't cling to him or cuddle him or flatter him or do or say any of the things that would have given her true feelings away. She had decided that she was happy to give him time to come to terms with their new relationship…as long as he was faithful.

The thought that he might not have been, that he might already have betrayed her trust in another woman's arms, threatened to tear Bee apart. In the circumstances he might even try to persuade her that he had assumed that their original agreement that he could have other women still held good. After all, Sergios thought fast on his feet and was, she reckoned ruefully, liable to fight dirty if she pushed him hard enough.

But Melita Thiarkis was a different kettle of fish. She was an islander, a local born and bred on Orestos, so Sergios had probably known her for a very long time. A fashion designer as well—no wonder he was so hung up on even his wife being stylish. There would be ties between Melita and Sergios stronger than Bee had ever wanted to consider. Melita was strikingly attractive rather than beautiful but very much the hot, sexy type likely to appeal to Sergios's high-voltage libido. The blonde was also confident of her place in Sergios's life, Bee recognised worriedly, recalling the way the other woman had looked her over without a shade of discomfort or concern. Melita, Bee reflected wretchedly, did not seem the slightest bit threatened by the fact that Sergios had recently got married. And what did that highly visible confidence signify? Had Sergios slept with his mistress since he had become Bee's husband?

As for the confirmation from Nectarios that Sergios's first marriage had been unhappy, Bee had long since worked that out for herself. The fact that there were no photos of Krista and her name was never mentioned had always suggested that that had been anything but a happy marriage. But Sergios, even though given every opportunity to do so, had still not chosen to confide that truth in Bee.

On the other hand, Bee reminded herself doggedly, she *had* been really happy and contented until she laid eyes on Melita Thiarkis and realised that temptation lived less than a mile from their door. Sergios, after all, had been remarkably attentive since they had first made love, but how could Bee possibly know what he got from his relationship with Melita? That he had insisted Melita was a non-negotiable feature of his life even *before* their marriage suggested the blonde had very good reason to be confident.

He did have a thing for blondes even though he wouldn't admit it, Bee thought bitterly as she peered at her dark brown locks in the bedroom mirror and tried to imagine herself transformed into a blonde. It would be sad to dye her hair just for his benefit, wouldn't it? Just at that moment of pain and stark fear she discovered that she didn't care if it was sad or not and she decided that she might well return from London with a mane of pretty blonde hair.

CHAPTER NINE

'I THOUGHT you would be in bed,' Sergio admitted when he landed in a helicopter after eleven that evening and strolled into the house. His tie was loosened and he was unshaven, his stunning eyes shadowed with tiredness. His sense of relief at being home again was intense and it startled him. 'It's been a long day and we have an early flight to London tomorrow morning.'

Bee glanced at him in surprise. 'You're coming with us?'

'Eleni's having surgery,' he reminded her with a frown. 'Of course I'm coming. Didn't you realise that?'

'No, I didn't.'

Delighted by his readiness to be supportive, Bee resisted the urge to immediately dredge up Melita's presence on the island. After all, if the blonde had a home and relatives on Orestos, she had a perfect right to visit and it might have nothing to do with Sergios. Was that simply wishful thinking? Bee asked herself as she put together a light supper in the big professional kitchen. She saw no need to disturb the staff so late when she was perfectly capable of feeding Sergios with her own fair hands.

He came out of his bathroom with a towel wrapped round his hips and sat down at the small table she had set up for his use. With his black hair flopping damply above his face and clean shaven, he looked less weary.

'Was it a difficult day?' Bee prompted uncertainly.

'It's always difficult.' Sergios grimaced and suddenly shrugged, acknowledging that it no longer felt reasonable to continue to keep Beatriz in the dark when it came to the touchy subject of his first marriage. 'Krista's parents remember a young woman I never knew, or maybe the young woman they talk about is the imaginary daughter they would have *liked* to have had—she certainly bears no resemblance to the woman I was married to for three years.'

Bee was confused. 'I don't understand...'

'Krista was a manic depressive and she loathed taking medication, didn't like what the prescribed tablets did to her. I didn't know about that when I married her. To be fair I hardly knew her when I asked her to marry me,' Sergios confided with a harsh edge to his dark deep drawl. 'I was young and stupid.'

'Oh.' Bee was so shattered about what his silence on the subject of his first wife had concealed that she could think of nothing else to say. A manic depressive? That was a serious condition but treatable with the right medical attention and support.

'I fell in love and rushed Krista to the altar, barely able to believe that the girl of my dreams was mine. Unfortunately the dream turned sour for us both,' he volunteered grittily, his face grim. 'As she refused medication there was no treatment that made an appreciable

difference to her moods. For most of our marriage she
was out of control. She took drugs and threw wild par-
ties before crashing drunk at the wheel of one of my
cars. She died instantly.'

'I am so sorry, Sergios,' Bee whispered with rich
sympathy, her heart truly hurting for him. 'So very
sorry you had to go through that and lose your child
into the bargain.'

'The baby wasn't mine. I don't know who fathered
the baby she was carrying at the time of her death.' His
handsome mouth twisted. 'By then we hadn't shared a
bed for a long time.'

'I wish you'd shared this with me sooner.' Bee was
still struggling to accept his wounding admission of
how much he had loved Krista, for she had convinced
herself that Sergios didn't know *how* to love a woman.
Now she was finding out different and it hurt her pride.

'I've always felt guilty that Krista died. I should've
been able to do more to help her.'

'How could you when she wouldn't accept that her
condition needed treatment?' Bee prompted quietly as
she got into bed and rested back against the pillows.
'Didn't her parents have any influence over her?'

'She was an adored only child. They were incapable
of telling her no and they refused to recognise the grav-
ity of her problems. Ultimately they blamed me for her
unhappiness.'

Striding restively about the room, his stunning eyes
bleak with distressing memories and his strong jaw line
clenched, he finally told her what his life had been like
with Krista. When he came home to the apartment he

had shared with his late wife in Athens back then he had never known what would greet him there. Violent disputes and upsetting scenes were a daily occurrence, as were his wife's periods of deep depression. Krista had done everything from shopping to partying to excess. On various occasions he had found her in bed with other men and high as a kite on the illegal drugs that she was convinced relieved her condition better than the proper medication. Staff walked out, friends were offended, the apartment was trashed and valuable objects were stolen. For three long years as he struggled to care for his deeply troubled wife Sergios had lived a life totally out of his own control and the love he had started out with had died. Bee finally understood why he had been so determined to have a businesslike marriage, which demanded nothing from him but financial input. He had put everything he had into his first marriage and it had still failed miserably. Krista had betrayed him and hurt him and taught him to avoid getting too deeply attached to anyone.

'Now you know why I never mention her,' Sergios murmured ruefully, sliding into bed beside her. 'I let her down so badly.'

'Krista was ill. You should forgive her and yourself for everything that went wrong,' Bee reasoned. 'You did your best and that's the most that anyone can do.'

Eyes level, Sergios lifted a hand and traced the full curve of her lower lip with a considering fingertip. 'You always say the right thing to make people feel better.'

Insanely conscious of his touch as she was, her heart

was galloping and her mouth had run dry. 'Do I?' she asked gruffly.

'When Paris asked you if his mother was in heaven you said yes even though you know she was an atheist, *moli mou*.'

'She still could have made it there in the end,' Bee reasoned without hesitation. 'Paris was worrying about it. I wanted him to have peace of mind.'

'I should've told you about Krista a long time ago but I hate talking about her—it feels wrong.'

'I understand why now and naturally you want to be loyal to her memory.' Melita's name was on the tip of her tongue but she could not bring herself to destroy that moment of closeness with suspicion and potential conflict. That conversation about Krista was quite enough for one evening.

'So sweet, so tactful…' Sergios leant closer, his breath fanning her cheek, and pried her lips apart with the tip of his tongue. With one kiss he could make her ache unbearably for the heat and hardness of his body.

'Someone round here has to be,' she teased, her breath rasping in her throat.

His tongue explored her tender mouth in an erotic foray and her nipples tingled into prominence. Desire slivered through her then, sharp as a blade. He freed her of the silk nightdress, cupping her breasts with firm hands, stroking the prominent pink crests with ravishing skill. She gasped beneath his mouth as he found the heated core of her and he made a sound of deep masculine satisfaction when he discovered how ready she was.

He turned her round and rearranged her, firm hands

cupping her hips as he plunged into her velvety depths with irresistible force and potency. He growled with pleasure above her head and pulled her back hard against him as he slowly rotated his hips to engulf her in an exquisite wash of sensation. While he pumped in and out of her he teased her clitoris with expert fingers. A soul-shattering climax gripped Bee as the tightening knot of heat inside her expanded and then exploded like a blazing star. Shaking and sobbing with pleasure, she fell back against him, weak as a kitten and drained of every thought and feeling.

'Go to sleep,' Sergios urged then, both arms still wrapped round her damp, trembling body. 'You'll exhaust yourself fretting about Eleni tomorrow.'

That he should know her so well almost made her laugh but she was too tired to find amusement in anything. Worry about Melita and Eleni and the passion had exhausted her and she fell heavily asleep.

Her first night back in London, Bee spent with her mother, who was both excited and apprehensive about her approaching move to Greece. Eleni was admitted to hospital the next morning. Both a nurse and the surgeon had talked Bee through every step of the entire procedure, which was likely to take less than an hour to complete, but Bee remained as nervous as a cat on hot bricks on Eleni's behalf, particularly because the little girl was too young to be prepared for the discomfort that might follow the surgery.

'We've already discussed all this,' Sergios reminded Bee firmly, very much a rock in the storm of her concern and anxiety. 'There is very little risk attached to this procedure and she will recover quickly from it. It may not improve her hearing but she is falling so far behind with her speech that it is worth a try.'

Cradling Eleni's solid little body in her lap with protective arms, Bee blinked back tears that embarrassed her for she had long since decided that surgery was currently the best treatment available. 'She's just so little and trusting.'

'Like you were when you married me,' Sergios quipped with a rueful grin, startling her with that light-hearted sally. 'You really didn't have a clue what you were signing up for but it hasn't turned out too bad for you, has it?'

'Ask me that in a year's time,' Bee advised, in no mood to stroke his ego.

'What a very begrudging response when I'm trying so hard to be the perfect husband!' he mocked.

Bee looked up at his handsome face and felt her heart leap like a dizzy teenager's. The perfect husband? Since when? And why? She had made no complaints, so it could not be her he was trying to influence. Most probably he was trying to please his grandfather, who was openly keen to see his only surviving grandson settling down with a family. But she didn't want Sergios putting on an act purely to impress Nectarios. Anything of that nature was almost certain to make Sergios feel deprived of free choice and she did not want their marriage to feel like an albatross hanging round his neck.

Bee accompanied Eleni to the very doors of the operating theatre and then waited outside with Sergios. He had taken the whole day off, which really surprised her. It was true that he stepped out several times to make and receive phone calls and that a PA brought documents for his signature, but it was so unusual for him to put work second that she was very appreciative of his continuing support.

The surgery was completed quickly and successfully and Bee took a seat by Eleni's bed. By that stage the little girl was already regaining consciousness. While she was groggy she was not, it seemed, in pain and, reassured by Bee's presence at her bedside, she soon drifted off to sleep. One of the nannies arrived to sit with the child while Sergios took Bee out for a meal and a much-needed break.

'You're exhausted. Why do I employ a team of nannies only to find you in this state? Come home with me,' Sergios urged when Bee's head began to nod towards the latter stages of their meal.

Her eyes widened and she studied him ruefully. 'I should be there if Eleni wakes up again and there is a bed in the room for me to use,' she reminded him. 'I won't have an entirely sleepless night.'

'Sometimes you should put yourself first,' Sergios reasoned levelly.

Bee tensed at that declaration and lost colour. Would he tell himself that when he felt the need for something a little more exotic than the marital bed could offer him? Would boredom or lust be his excuse? Would he even need an excuse or was sex with Melita already so familiar that it would not feel like a betrayal of his marital vows? She studied his features: the level line of his brows, the stunning dark golden eyes above those blade-straight cheekbones and the wide carnal mouth that could transport her to paradise. Her cheeks burned as she tore her attention from him. She should challenge him about Melita. Why wasn't she doing that? When would there ever be a *right* moment for such a distressing confrontation?

When Eleni was lying in a hospital bed was definitely not the right time, she decided unhappily. That conversation was not something she wanted to plunge blindly into either. She needed to know exactly what she planned to say and right at that instant it felt like too emotive a subject for her to maintain a level head. She didn't want to shout or cry. She was determined to retain her dignity. After all she was in love with him and at the end of the day dignity might be all she had left to embrace, along with the empty shell of her marriage as they both retired behind their respective barriers. Would they ever share a bed again after that conversation?

'What's wrong?' Sergios demanded abruptly. 'You look haunted. Eleni's going to be fine. Stop doing this to yourself. It was a straightforward procedure and it went perfectly.'

'I know…I'm sorry. I think I'm just tired,' Bee muttered evasively, embarrassed that he could read her well enough to know that she was currently existing in a sort of mental hell. Melita was a sexy stunner; there was no getting round that hard fact. Every man in the taverna between fifteen and eighty-odd years had been staring appreciatively at the racy blonde. Just at that instant Bee could not forget, humiliatingly, that she had had to get half naked and swing provocatively round a pole to tempt her highly sexed and sophisticated husband into making their marriage a real one.

'You worry far too much about stuff.' Sergios shook his handsome dark head in emphasis. 'It's like you're always on the lookout for trouble.'

Bee was back by Eleni's bed when her cell phone vibrated silently in receipt of a text and she took it out of her jacket pocket, wondering wearily if it would be Jon Townsend again. Once he knew she would be over in London he had asked her to lunch with key charity personnel. Too concerned about Eleni's needs to spare the time for such an occasion, Bee had hedged. But it was not Jon texting her this time…

I'm in London. I would like to meet you in private. *Melita.*

Aghast at the idea while noting that the word private was emphasised, Bee looked at her phone as though it had jumped up and bitten her. Her husband's mistress was actually texting her? Was it for real? But for what possible reason would anyone try to set Bee up with a fake text purporting to be from Melita? Assuming the text was genuine, how on earth had Melita Thiarkis got Bee's phone number? Had she taken it from Sergios's phone? It was the most likely explanation and as such hit Bee's spirits hard because it was not long since she had got a new number and if Melita was in possession of it, it suggested very recent contact between Sergios and the other woman.

Bee got little sleep that night although Eleni slept like a little snoring log. Sergios put in an appearance on his way into his London office. Bee was in the corridor and noticed the ripple of interest that her extraordinarily good-looking husband excited among the nursing staff. With his tall, wide-shouldered, long-legged frame encased in a charcoal-grey designer suit, Sergios looked spectacular. Eleni was equally impressed and whooped with glee when he came through the door and held out her arms.

An odd little smile softened the hard line of Sergios's mouth as he set down the package in his hand. Bending down, he scooped the little girl gently out of her bed, addressing her in Greek as he did so.

And for the very first time Eleni answered, looking up at him with big dark eyes. The words were indistinct and the sentence structure non-existent, but it was a response she would not have attempted before the surgery.

'I noticed she was more attentive to what I was saying from the minute she woke up this morning,' Bee told him with forced brightness. 'She's definitely able to hear more. Her eyes don't wander the same way when you're speaking to her either.'

Bee helped Eleni unwrap the wooden puzzle that Sergios had brought and pulled up the bed table for the little girl's use. A ward maid popped her head round the door and offered them a cup of coffee.

'Not for me, thanks,' Sergios responded. 'I have an early meeting.'

'If her consultant thinks everything is in order, Eleni will be released later this afternoon,' Bee revealed.

'Good. The boys missed you last night,' Sergios told her.

If he had told her that *he* had missed her she would have thrown herself into his arms like a homing pigeon, but no such encouraging declaration passed his lips. Nor would it, Bee reflected wretchedly. Sergios didn't say sentimental stuff like that or make emotional statements. She loved a guy who would never ever tell her he loved her back. And why would he settle solely for Bee's charms when he already had a woman like Melita and countless other discreet lovers eternally on offer to him? He was an immensely wealthy tycoon and, when it came to women and sex, spoilt for choice and it would always be that way. Somehow, she didn't know yet *how*, she would have to come to terms with the reality of their marriage. Possibly meeting Melita Thiarkis in the flesh would be a sensible first step in that much-needed process.

That decision made, Sergios had barely left the building before Bee texted the other woman to set up the requested meeting. After all, what did she have to lose? Sergios wouldn't like the idea of them meeting at all but why should that bother her? He would never find out, would he? Had he chosen to be more frank about the relationship, however, Bee would probably have ignored the text from his mistress. Melita replied immediately and asked Bee to meet her in the bar of her Chelsea hotel mid-morning. Wary of staging such a delicate encounter in a public place, Bee suggested she come to her room instead.

Bee would very much have liked her entire designer wardrobe on hand to choose from before she met up with Melita. But, travelling direct from the hospital, that was not possible and Bee, not only had very little choice about what to wear, but despised the vain streak of insecurity that had prompted such a superficial thought. She could hardly hope to top a fashion designer in the style stakes, she told herself wryly as she freshened up her make-up and left Eleni with her nanny for company. Pausing only to tell her security team of two that she did not require them, she walked out of the hospital.

The receptionist sent her straight up to Melita's room on the first floor. She knocked only once on the door before it opened to frame the strikingly attractive woman, who even at that point impressed Bee as being vastly overdressed for morning coffee in her low-cut glittering jacket, narrow skirt and very high heels.

'Beatriz…' Melita murmured smoothly. 'I'm so grateful that you agreed to come, but let's not tell Sergios about this. Men hate it when we go behind their backs.'

CHAPTER TEN

BEE took due note of the fact that her husband's mistress, Melita, was more scared of consequences than she was. As Bee had no intention of keeping their meeting a secret unless it suited her to do so, she did not reply.

Melita already had a pot of coffee waiting in her opulent hotel room with its black and white designer chic decor. She sat down opposite Bee, a process that took a good deal of cautious lowering and wriggling in six-inch heels and a black skirt so tight it would split if put under too much pressure. Melita walked a thin line between sexy and tarty.

'I didn't think that Sergios would ever marry again,' the Greek woman said plaintively. 'But we're adults. There's no reason why we can't be, er…distant friends.'

Only one, Bee completed inwardly. *If you sleep with my husband I might try to murder you.*

'Sergios and I have been very close for a great many years,' Melita informed her with a self-satisfied smile.

Not a muscle moving on her taut face, Bee compressed her lips and pretended to sip at the too-hot coffee that Melita had poured for her. 'I guessed that.'

'I have no intention of poaching on your territory,'

Melita declared importantly. 'I've never wanted to be a wife or a mother, so I don't covet what you have.'

'But you do covet Sergios,' Bee heard herself say helplessly.

'*Any* woman would covet him,' the other woman fielded, her sultry eyes widening in amused emphasis. 'But there's no reason why we can't share him.'

'Just one,' Bee murmured flatly. 'I *don't* share.'

Melita's pencilled brows drew together in surprise at that bold statement. 'Is that a declaration of war?'

'It's whatever you choose to make of it. Why did you invite me here?' Bee enquired drily.

'I wanted to reassure you that I have no desire to damage your marriage. Sergios really does need a wife to do wifely things like looking after his houses and his children. Naturally I'm aware that it is a marriage of… shall we say…' Melita looked unconvincingly coy for a moment '…mutual convenience?'

'Oh, dear…is that what Sergios told you?' Bee asked, wincing with an acting ability she had not known she possessed, for she refused to cringe at the apparent level of Melita's knowledge about Sergios's reasons for marrying her. 'Men can be so reluctant to break bad news. I'm afraid our marriage is rather more than one of convenience.'

'If by that you mean that Sergios shares your bed, I expected that. After all you're there when I can't be and he's a man, very much a man,' Melita purred with glinting eyes of sensual recollection.

For a split second Bee felt so sick that she almost ran into the en suite and lost her sparse hospital breakfast.

She could not bear to think of Melita naked and intimately wound round Sergios. That *hurt*, that hurt like a punch in the stomach. Nor could she bear to consider herself a sexual substitute, a sort of cheap and available fast-food option instead of the grand banquet of thrilling sensuality that she imagined Melita might offer.

'You do realise, I hope, that your husband is still shagging me every chance he gets!' Dropping the civilised front with a resounding crash, Melita surveyed Bee with angry, resentful dark eyes. 'He was with me on your wedding night and I have no intention of giving him up.'

'Whatever,' Bee framed woodenly, setting down the cup with precise care and rising to her feet again with all the dignity she could muster. 'I think we've shared a little too much for comfort. If you contact me again I'll tell Sergios.'

'Don't you dare threaten me!' Melita ranted furiously.

Bee walked out and she didn't look back or breathe until she was safe inside the lift again. Sergios was still sleeping with his mistress and had been from the first night of their marriage. Why was she so shocked? What else had she expected? That a man with a notoriously active libido would suddenly turn over a new leaf on entering a platonic marriage? That had never been a possibility. Before their marriage she had agreed to him maintaining his relationship with Melita. He had said upfront that Melita was not a negotiable facet of his life. Having received that warning, she had chosen to ignore it by allowing their marriage to become much more real than either of them had ever envisaged.

Leaving the hotel, Bee was blank-eyed, her mind in chaos and emotions raging through her in horribly distressing waves. She didn't know where she was going but she knew she couldn't return to the hospital in such a state, nor would she involve her mother when she was so upset. Her cell phone was ringing and she checked it. It was Jon Townsend. Heaving a sigh, but in a strange way grateful for the distraction, Bee answered his call. He invited her to join him at his apartment for lunch with the charity's PR woman. It was somewhere to go, something to do in a world rocking on its foundations, and she agreed and boarded a bus, too wrapped in her own unhappy thoughts to notice that she was being followed.

Sergios had already cancelled appointments and left his office, planning to meet with Beatriz at the hospital. The news that she had met up with Melita had hit him like a torpedo and almost blown him out of the water. Where had that come from? How had that happened? What had he done to deserve that outcome? Nourishing a strong sense of injustice along with the suspicion that he was being royally stitched up, Sergios was in no mood to receive the bodyguard's second piece of news: Beatriz had entered an apartment owned by Jon Townsend?

'Beatriz...' From the minute Bee stepped through the door, she began regretting having agreed to lunch. Jon was alone, the PR lady apparently having been held up in traffic. Unfortunately her host's effusive welcome made Bee feel even more awkward.

Bee toyed with the salad on her plate and for the third time attempted to steer their conversation back to the subject of the charity and away from the past times that Jon seemed much more eager to discuss.

'We were so close back then.' Jon sighed fondly.

'Not as close as I thought at the time. We *were* still very young,' Bee pointed out lightly.

'I didn't realise how much you meant to me until it was too late and I'd lost you,' Jon said baldly.

'It happens.' Her attempted smile of acknowledgement was a mere twist of her lips, for she was in no frame of mind to deal tactfully with Jon's evident determination to resurrect their shared past. 'If you had been happy with me you wouldn't have strayed.'

Jon brought a hand down on top of hers and she was so irritated with him that she very nearly lifted her other hand to stab him with the fork. 'Jenna—'

Bee lifted a hand to silence him. 'Stop right there. I really don't want to hear about your marriage, Jon. It's none of my business.'

'Perhaps I want to make it your business.'

'More probably you're barking up the wrong tree— I'm in love with my husband,' Bee responded impatiently. 'And now I think it's time I went. I want to get back to the hospital.'

As she got up Jon leapt up as well and the doorbell went in one long shrill shriek as if the caller's finger had accidentally got stuck to the button.

'A shame your PR lady is arriving so late,' Bee remarked.

'That was just a ruse, Bee,' Jon snapped, his fair features twisting with bad temper and momentarily giving him the aspect of a disgruntled little boy.

'Evidently, Sergios was right to tell me that I'm too trusting,' Bee was saying as Jon angrily yanked open the front door, annoyed by the timely interruption.

Bee was totally shattered to see Sergios poised on the doorstep. 'What are you doing here?' she asked in astonishment. 'How did you find out where I was?'

His eyes had a smouldering glitter and were welded to Jon's discomfited face. 'Why did my wife say that I was right to call her too trusting?'

Bee really couldn't be bothered with Jon at that moment. The whole silly lunch set-up had thoroughly irritated her, but she didn't want Sergios to thump him. And that, she sensed, very much aware of the powerfully angry aggression Sergios exuded, was quite likely if she didn't act to defuse the tension.

'I was just joking. We were discussing a charity dinner—'

Sergios closed a hand round her wrist and drew her out of the apartment as if he couldn't wait to remove her from a source of dangerous contagion. His face hard as iron, he studied Jon, who was pale and taut. 'Leave my wife alone,' he instructed with chilling bite. 'What's mine stays mine. Try not to forget that.'

What's mine stays mine. Bee could have been very sarcastic about that assurance had she not been outraged by Sergios's intervention and sexist turn of phrase.

'Sometimes you're very dramatic,' she commented lamely, recognising that quality in him for the first time and surprised by the discovery.

'What were you doing in Townsend's apartment alone with him?' Sergios shot at her, visibly unrepentant.

'None of your business.'

As the lift doors opened on the ground floor Sergios shot Bee an arrested look. 'Explain yourself.'

'Are we going to pick up Eleni?' Bee enquired coldly instead, picturing Melita with her smug cat-got-the-cream smile. Nausea pooled in her tummy again and turned her skin clammy.

'Eleni was released an hour ago. Karen phoned me and I told her to take Eleni home.'

'Oh.' Bee made no further comment, stabbed by guilt that she had forgotten the little girl was due to leave hospital that afternoon. She felt drained by the emotional storm of the past couple of hours. The man she loved had a mistress whom he regularly slept with and would not give up. Where did she go from there? Did she really want to lower herself to the level of arguing about Melita? Did she want to run the risk of exposing how deep her own feelings went for him?

Or did she do the sensible thing? Take it on the chin and move on? Obviously no more sharing of marital beds. That kind of intimacy was out of the question with Melita in the picture. But she had signed up to a long-term relationship for the sake of her mother and for the children. Every fibre of her being might be urging her to make some sort of grand gesture like walking out on her marriage, but too many innocent people would be hurt and damaged by her doing that. Even Sergios had said that she wasn't a quitter and he had been right on that score. She gave her word and, my goodness, she stuck to it through thick and thin.

Even through Melita? Could she still stick to her word in such circumstances? Pain slivered through Bee and cut deep like a knife. They had roamed so far from their original agreement. Far too many tender feelings had got involved. Stepping back from that intimacy, learning to be detached again would be a huge challenge, she acknowledged wretchedly. Had she really once believed that she could treat Sergios like a rather demanding employer? Looking at Sergios's beloved face now, she was no longer sure that she had the strength to stand by her promise and survive the sacrifices that that would demand.

How could she bear to turn her back on what she had believed they had and know that Melita was replacing her in every way that mattered? From now on it would be Melita he kissed awake in the morning, Melita he took to dine in cosy little restaurants where nobody recognised him, Melita he bought whopping big diamonds for. How could Bee live with knowing that he had only made love to her because she was there when more tempting sexual prospects were not? What had meant so much to her had evidently meant very little to him. A cry of anguish was building up inside Bee. She felt as though she were being ripped apart.

The limo came to a halt. White-faced, she got out without even looking to see where she was going and came to a sudden bemused halt once she realised that they had not alighted at the mansion that was their London home but outside an apartment building she had never seen before. 'Where are we?'

'I own an apartment here.'

'Oh...do you?' she queried drily, wondering if this was where he had come on their wedding night to make love with his Greek blonde. She was ready to bet that he had not had to nudge Melita towards the sexy lingerie. Gut instinct warned her that Melita already had that kind of angle covered, or uncovered, as regarded his preference, she thought bitterly. Had she seriously considered dying her hair blonde? Had she really been that pathetic? Where had her pride and her independence gone?

Love had decimated those traits, she decided painfully, standing, lost and sick to the soul, in the lift on the way up to the apartment she had not known he possessed. Love had made her hollow and weak inside. Love had made her want to cling and dye her hair and wear the fancy lingerie if that was what it took to hold him. But her brain told her that that was nonsense and that those were only superficial frills, not up to the challenge of keeping a doomed relationship afloat. And a relationship between plain, ordinary, sensible Bee Blake and rich and gorgeous Sergios Demonides had always been doomed, hadn't it? A union between two such different people was unlikely to be a marriage that ran and ran against all the odds...unless you believed in miracles and wild dreams coming true. And

Bee had so *badly* wanted to believe that she could have the miracle, the dream.

Virtually blind to her surroundings while that ferocity of emotion remained in control of her, Bee preceded Sergios into a spacious lounge that had that slightly bare, unlived in quality of a property not in daily use. 'So this is where you and Melita—'

Sergios froze in front of her as though she had said a very bad word, his face clenching hard, sensual mouth compressing. 'No, not here. My grandfather uses this place when he visits London—he likes his independence. It's a company property.'

Bee nodded and her spine relaxed just a jot. She had conceived a loathing for Melita Thiarkis, everywhere the other woman had ever been with Sergios and everything to do with her that was excessive to say the least.

'She's never been here—she has her own apartment,' Sergios breathed abruptly as if he were attuned to Bee's every thought.

Never having had quite so many mean, malicious thoughts all at once, Bee seriously hoped that he was not that attuned. Her disconcerted face was hot, her complexion flushed to the hairline with embarrassment and the distress she was fighting to conceal. Suddenly unable to bear looking at him, she spun away and faked an interest in the view.

'Whatever it takes I want to keep you,' Sergios breathed with startling harshness. 'I hope you appreciate the fact that I didn't knock Townsend's teeth down his throat the way I would've liked to have done.'

'You can be such a caveman.' In a twisty way that

appealed to the dark side of her temperament, she was painfully amused that despite his own extra-marital interests he could still be so possessive of *her*. The logic of his attitude escaped her. But, of course, he wanted to keep her as a wife: he needed her for the children. They loved her and she loved them. Now there had to be a compromise found that she and Sergios could both live with. Some magical solution that would provide a path through the messy swell of emotion currently blurring her view of the world.

'Look at me…' Sergios urged.

'I don't want to,' Bee said truthfully, but she turned round all the same.

She wondered why it was that she could now see that Jon sulked and pouted like a spoilt little boy when he didn't get his own way, but that in spite of what she had learned about Sergios she still could not see a visible flaw in him. He remained defiantly gorgeous from his stunning dark golden eyes to his slightly stubbled and shadowed chin.

'That's better,' he murmured, scrutinising her with an intensity that made her uncomfortable.

'Why did you bring me here?'

'If we're going to argue, if there's going to be dissension between us, I didn't want the children as an audience,' Sergios admitted flatly, features grave.

'My word, you think of everything!' Bee was all too wretchedly aware that she would not have considered that danger until it was too late.

'They deserve better from us—'

'Is that you reminding me of my duty?' Bee prompted tightly, her throat suddenly thickening with tears.

'Whatever it takes I want to hold onto you.'

'You already said that.'

'It's more than I've ever said to a woman,' Sergios breathed roughly, challenge in the stance of his big powerful body. He stood tall with broad shoulders thrown back and strong legs braced as though he were expecting a blow.

He wanted everything, he wanted too much, she reflected unhappily. He wanted his mistress and he wanted his wife, a combination he evidently believed necessary to his comfort and happiness. Emotion didn't come into it for him. If only it didn't come into it for her either! Her eyes prickled hotly and she kept them very wide, terrified that the tears threatening her would spill over in front of him.

'If we're staying here I could do with lying down for a while,' she said abruptly, desperate for some privacy.

'Of course.' He crossed the room and pressed open a door that led into a corridor. He showed her into the bedroom and startled her by yanking the bedspread off the bed and pulling back the duvet for her. He looked across at her, a dark uncertainty in his eyes that she had never seen before, and for the first time it occurred to her that he was upset as well.

'Thanks,' she said dully, taking off her jacket and kicking off her shoes.

'Would you like a drink?' he enquired without warning.

'A brandy,' she responded, dimly reca[...]

being recommended for shock in a book she had read. Probably not at all the right remedy for shock in today's world, she thought ruefully. In fact, couldn't alcohol act as a depressant? In the mood she was in, she didn't need that, did she?

Seemingly glad, however, of something to do, Sergios strode out of the room and she sat down on the bed. Time seemed to move on without her noticing, for he reappeared very quickly and handed her a tumbler half full of brandy. 'Are you trying to get me drunk?' she asked in disbelief.

'You look like a ghost, all white and drawn. Drink up,' Sergios urged.

'I can't live like this with you...' she framed, the admission leaping off her tongue before she could stop it.

Sergios came down on his knees at her feet and pushed the tumbler towards her mouth. 'Drink,' he urged again.

'It might make me sick.'

'I don't think so.'

All of a sudden she noticed that the hand he had on the glass was trembling almost infinitesimally. He was behaving as though the drink might be a lifesaver, rather than a pick-me-up. She sipped, shuddering as the alcohol ran like a flame down her throat, making her cough and splutter. She collided with strained dark eyes.

'...the heck is the matter with you?' Bee demanded in sudden frustration. 'You're behaving very

...upright. 'What do you expect? You ...mistress—then you run straight off to stage a private meeting with your ex, who's clearly desperate to get you back!' he exclaimed wrathfully. 'I mean, it's not exactly been my dream day and I still don't know what the hell is going on!'

Former mistress? Her ears were practically out on stalks. Was he planning to try and lie his way out of the tight corner he was in? Pretend that his relationship with Melita was over? While pondering that salient point, Bee drank deep of the brandy, grateful for the heat spreading and somehow soothing her cold, empty tummy.

'Why did you go and see Melita?' he demanded heavily. 'What the hell made you do such a thing?'

Her brow indented. 'She asked me to come and see her.'

His lean powerful face set granite hard at that claim. '*She* asked...*you*?'

Bee lifted her chin. 'Yes and I was curious. Of course I was. I saw her on the island last week.'

His gaze narrowed. 'Nectarios mentioned it but I hoped you didn't realise who she was.'

Bee rolled her eyes. 'I'm not stupid, Sergios.'

'Not obviously so,' he conceded. 'But if you believed I've been with her since we got married, you are being stupid.'

'According to Melita you've been shagging her every chance you got—that's a direct quote from her,' Bee told him.

Sergios looked astonished. 'I thought better of her. We parted—as I thought—on good terms.'

'When did you last see her?'

'About six weeks ago in Athens. We did not have sex,' Sergios added sardonically. 'I have not slept with her since we got married.'

Bee vented a scornful laugh. 'How am I supposed to believe that about the woman you insisted you had to keep in your life in spite of our marriage?'

'It's the truth. Melita was part of my routine.'

'Routine?' Bee repeated with distaste.

'It wasn't a romantic relationship. I financed her fashion house, she shared my bed. She travelled all round the world to meet up with me. It was easier keeping her as a mistress than having to adapt to different women,' Sergios admitted, his discomfort with the topic obvious. 'I've known her for a long time. I backed her first fashion collection because she was an islander. We ended up in bed after Krista died and I found Melita's casual approach to sex attractive at a time when I didn't want anything heavy.'

'If it was over why did she lie?'

'Presumably because she thought that if she could cause trouble between us I might come back to her,' Sergios suggested grimly. 'I'm furious that she approached you and lied to you. I made a generous settlement on her at the end of our affair and she should've been satisfied with that.'

'She said you were with her on our wedding night.'

He swore only half below his breath, anger burn-ing his gaze. 'I was supposed to see her but I

played the tables and drank.

Going to her didn't feel right. I know our marriage was supposed to be a fake but making a point of being with her that particular night...' Sergios shrugged uncomfortably. 'It would've felt disrespectful, so I didn't do it.'

'Disrespectful,' Bee echoed weakly, her attention nailed to his face, recognising the combination of discomfiture and sincerity she saw there.

'I swear I have not been with Melita,' Sergios growled, his patience taxed almost beyond its limits. 'And if I have to drag her here and make her admit that to your face, I will not shrink from the challenge.'

'She wouldn't come.'

'She would if I threatened to withdraw the settlement I made on her. She signed a legal agreement, promising to be discreet about our past relationship and approaching my wife and lying to her is not, by any stretch of the imagination, discreet!' he bit out thunderously, his anger at what he had learned unconcealed.

Bee recalled how very keen Melita had been to ensure that Sergios did not know about their meeting, hardly surprising if the money he had given her was dependent on her remaining tactfully silent about their affair. Was it possible that she had simply wanted to cause trouble? Naturally she would blame Bee for Sergios having broken off their relationship.

'I'm starting to believe you,' Bee confided with a frown, worried that she was being ridiculously credulous while at the same time recalling that she had yet to find out that Sergios had ever lied to her about anything. He was much more given to lethal candour than dishonesty.

'Thank God,' he breathed in Greek.

'But I still don't get why you were so determined to retain Melita that you even told me about her before the wedding…only to get rid of her a few weeks later.'

Sergios groaned like a man in torment. 'Obviously because I had you and didn't need her any longer.'

'Oh…' was all Bee could think to say to that. Was it really that simple for him? Instead of sex with Melita he had discovered sex with his wife and found it a perfectly adequate substitute? Seemingly it *was* that simple on his terms. It was a huge relief to appreciate that he had not betrayed her with Melita. Her head was swimming a little and she thought that perhaps she had had a little too much brandy.

'You're fantastic in bed, *yineka mou*.'

'Am I?' Bee settled big green eyes on him, wide with wonderment at that assurance.

'I haven't even looked at another woman since I married you,' Sergios spelt out forcefully. 'Nor will I in the future. That's a promise. Will you come home with me now?'

A huge smile was tugging the last of the stress from round her ripe mouth. 'You still haven't explained how you knew where I was this afternoon.'

'Your security team know not to listen to you if you try to go anywhere without them in tow. They followed you. What did Townsend want?'

'Me apparently, but after all this time I'm really not interested. I told him that I…er…' Bee hesitated at what she had almost revealed. 'I told Jon that I had become quite attached to you.'

'Attached? Is that a fact?' Sergios prompted softly, sitting down on the bed beside her and tucking her hair back behind one small ear with a gentle hand. 'I'm quite attached to you as well.'

'Sexually speaking,' Bee qualified, a glutton for accuracy.

'Well, I have to admit that you have the most fabulous breasts and I'm ashamed to admit that they are the first thing I noticed about you the night we met,' Sergios confessed with the beginnings of a wicked grin. 'But you've contrived to build whole layers on that initial impression. You're a great listener, marvellous company, very loyal, intelligent and affectionate. When I'm angry or stressed you make me feel calm. When I'm unkind you make me see another viewpoint. I'm not even mentioning how wonderful you are with the children because that's not what you and I are about any more—'

Bee went from hanging on his every flattering word to cutting in with a quick question. 'It's...*not*?'

'Of course, it's not. We started out with a practical marriage.'

'You told Melita that too, didn't you?' Bee recalled unhappily, her brow indenting with a remembered sense of humiliation.

His forefinger smoothed away the tension that had tightened her mouth. 'I'm afraid it slipped out but I really did believe we were going to have a marriage that was like a business deal.'

'And how do you feel now?' she whispered.

'Like I made the killing of a lifetime when I got you to the altar,' Sergios declared, his eyes warmer than she had ever seen them as he studied her intently. 'You've got to know how crazy I am about you. You taught me to love again. You taught me how to trust and you transformed my life.'

Bee stared at him wide-eyed. 'You're crazy about me?'

'I'm hopelessly in love with you.'

Bee wrapped both arms round him as though he were a very large teddy bear and dragged him down to her. 'I was trying to save face when I said I was attached to you.'

'I rather hoped that that was what you were doing, *agape mou*.'

'I love you too but I still don't know why.'

'Don't question it too closely in case you change your mind,' Sergios warned.

'It's just you weren't the most loveable guy around when we got married.'

'But I'm really working at it now,' he pointed out. 'And I won't stop.'

Bee studied him with bemused green eyes. 'You promise?'

'I promise. I love you. All I want is to make you happy.'

The sincerity in his liquid dark gaze went straight to her impressionable heart and tears stung the backs of her eyes. Finally, she believed him. Their marriage was safe. Even better, he was hers in exactly the way she had dreamed. He loved her and love was, she sensed, the only chain that would hold him.

'I should've known I was in trouble when I bought that wedding dress,' Sergios confided with a rueful laugh.

'What were you doing at a fashion show?' As he winced she guessed the answer. 'You were there because of Melita and yet you picked a dress for me?' she prompted in amazement.

'I saw the dress and I couldn't help picturing you wearing it and I know it was high-handed of me but I was determined that you should have it,' Sergios revealed.

She was touched by the admission that even before their wedding he had been attracted to her to that extent. 'Yet we both thought that I was going to be more of an employee than a real wife.'

'Even I can be stupid.'

Bee grinned with appreciation. 'Hold on while I get a microphone and record that statement.'

'Well, I was stupid about you. I was fighting what I felt for you right from the start.'

'Your marriage to Krista hurt you a great deal,' Bee commented softly, understanding that and willing to forgive the time it had taken for him to recognise his feelings for her.

'I thought I would be happier living without a serious relationship in my life. You rewrote everything I thought I knew about myself. I wanted you. I wanted you in my bed, my home, involved in every aspect of my day.' Sergios circled her mouth slowly, gently, with his. 'I know I didn't tell you that I'd finished with Melita but I didn't see the need.'

'I thought that maybe you thought you could still have both of us.'

Unexpectedly, Sergios laughed. 'No, I was never that stupid. I knew that wasn't an option but possibly I felt a little foolish about changing my mind so quickly and wanting the kind of marriage I said I definitely didn't want.'

Bee brushed a high cheekbone with gentle fingertips, loving the new confidence powering her. 'That aspect never occurred to me.'

'It should've done. I thought I had our marriage all worked out and it blew up in my face because I couldn't keep my hands off you.'

'When I saw Melita I decided you only liked blondes…and for just a little while I actually considered getting my hair dyed. It was my lowest moment,' Bee confided with a wince of shame.

Sergios groaned out loud, his long fingers feathering through her glossy dark hair. 'I'm very grateful you didn't do it. I love your hair the way it is—'

'I might grow it longer for you,' Bee proffered, feeling unusually generous.

Sergios pressed her back against the pillows and extracted a kiss that was full of hungry urgency. 'Now that we're here, we might as well take advantage.'

'Oh, yes,' Bee agreed, full pink lips swollen, eyes wide with desire as the tug of arousal pinched low in her tummy.

And the kissing shifted into a fairly wild bout of lovemaking. Afterwards, Bee lay in her husband's arms, feeling loved and secure and boundlessly happy and grateful for what she had.

On the drive back to their London home that evening, Sergios dealt her a slightly embarrassed appraisal and said abruptly, 'I thought that possibly in a few months' time we might consider having a baby.'

'On the grounds that we've got so many children we might as well have another?' Bee prompted very drily.

Sergios grimaced. 'I suppose I deserve that reminder but I've changed. I would like to have a child with you some day in the future.'

'I can agree to that now you've got the right attitude,' Bee told him chirpily and she flung herself into his arms with abandon and snuggled close. 'And now I know that you love me, you had better get used to me doing stuff like this.'

His strong arms enfolded her and dark golden eyes rested on her animated face with tender appreciation. 'And maybe I've even learned to like it, *yineka mou*.'

Bee relaxed and knew she could hug him to her heart's content. From here on in there would be no more boundaries she feared to cross.

EPILOGUE

'How do you feel?' Sergios asked, his anxiety obvious.

'Absolutely fine!' Bee exclaimed, widening her bright eyes in reproach. 'Stop fussing!'

But Bee was less than pleased with her reflection in the mirror. It was Nectarios's eighty-third birthday and they were throwing a big party for the older man at their home on the island. She was wearing a beautiful evening gown in one of her favourite colours but, it had to be said, nothing, not even the fabulous diamonds glittering in her ears and at her throat, could make her elegant in her own eyes while she was heavily pregnant. At almost eight months pregnant with their first child, she felt like a ship in full sail.

Sergios drew her back against him, his hands splaying gently across her swollen abdomen, his fascination palpable as he felt the slight ripple of movement as their daughter kicked. A little girl, that was what they were having according to the most recent sonogram. Eleni was four years old and she was very excited about the baby sister who would soon be born. Bee had enjoyed furnishing a nursery and had frittered away many a happy hour choosing baby equipment and clothing.

Bee, however, could hardly believe that she and Sergios had been married for going on for three years. They had waited a little longer than they had originally planned to try for a baby but she had conceived quickly. There was not a single cloud in Bee's sky. The previous year, Melita Thiarkis had sold her island property and set up permanent home in Milan with an Italian millionaire. Bee had never got involved with the charity Jon Townsend had worked with because he made her uncomfortable, but she had picked another charity, one that concentrated on disabled adults like her mother. When she was not running round after the children or travelling with Sergios, for they did not like to be kept apart for more than a couple of nights, she put in sterling work seeking out sponsors for the organisation and raising funds.

Bee's mother, Emilia was firmly settled now in her cottage on Orestos. Happier and healthier than she had been for several years, the older woman was fully integrated into island life and a good deal less lonely and bored. She loved living close to her daughter and took great pleasure in Paris, Milo and Eleni running in and out of her house and treating her as an honorary grandmother. Nectarios was a regular visitor to his grandson's home and a very welcome one. He was thrilled that his fourth great-grandchild was on the way.

'You've made so many arrangements for this party. I don't want you to tire yourself out,' Sergios admitted.

The house was full of guests and there was a distant hum, which probably signified the approach of another helicopter ready to drop off more guests.

'I'll be fine.' Bee was wryly amused by the level of his concern, for she had enjoyed a healthy pregnancy that had impinged very little on her usual routine. He was so supportive though, having rigorously attended every medical appointment with her.

Sergios studied the woman he loved and once again worked to suppress his secret fear of the idea of anything ever happening to her. The more he loved her, the more central she became to his world, and the more he worried but the bottom line, the payoff, he had learned, was a level of love and contentment he had never known until she entered his life.

'I love you, *agape mou*,' he murmured gently at the top of the sweeping staircase.

Bee met his stunning dark golden eyes and felt the leap of every sense with happy acceptance. The world they had made together was a safe cocoon for both them and the children. 'I love you more than I could ever say.'

* * * * *

CLASSIC

REQUEST YOUR
FREE BOOKS!

2 FREE NOVELS PLUS
2 FREE GIFTS!

*The legacy of the powerful
Sicilian Ferrara dynasty continues in
THE FORBIDDEN FERRARA
by USA TODAY bestselling author Sarah Morgan.*

Enjoy this sneak peek!

A Ferrara would never sit down at a Baracchi table for fear of being poisoned.

Fia had no idea why Santo was here. He didn't know.

He *couldn't* know.

"*Buona sera,* Fia."

A deep male voice came from the doorway, and she turned. The crazy thing was, she didn't know his voice. But she knew his eyes and they were looking at her now—two dark pools of dangerous black. They gleamed bright with intelligence and hard with ruthless purpose. They were the eyes of a man who thrived in a cutthroat business environment. A man who knew what he wanted and wasn't afraid to go after it. They were the same eyes that had glittered into hers in the darkness three years before as they'd ripped each other's clothes and slaked a fierce hunger.

He was exactly the same. Still the same "born to rule" Ferrara self-confidence; the same innate sophistication, polished until it shone bright as the paintwork of his Lamborghini.

She wanted him to go to hell and stay there.

He was her biggest mistake.

And judging from the cold, cynical glint in his eye, he considered her to be his.

"Well, this is a surprise. The Ferrara brothers don't usually step down from their ivory tower to mingle with us mortals. Checking out the competition?" She adopted her

Harlequin®

Romance

A touching new duet from fan-favorite author

SUSAN MEIER

First Time DADS!

When millionaire CEO Max Montgomery spots Kate Hunter-Montgomery—the wife he's never forgotten—back in town with a daughter who looks just like him, he's determined to win her back. But can this savvy business tycoon convince Kate to trust him a second time with her heart?

Find out this June in

THE TYCOON'S SECRET DAUGHTER

And look for book 2 coming this August!

NANNY FOR THE
MILLIONAIRE'S TWINS

Saddle up with Harlequin® series books this summer and find a cowboy for every mood!

most businesslike tone, while all the time her anxiety was rising and the questions were pounding through her head.

Did he know?

Had he found out?

A faint smile touched his mouth and the movement distracted her. There was an almost deadly beauty in the sensual curve of those lips. Everything about the man was dark and sexual, as if he'd been designed for the express purpose of drawing women to their doom. If rumor were correct, he did that with appalling frequency.

Fia wasn't fooled by his apparently relaxed pose or his deceptively mild tone.

Santo Ferrara was the most dangerous man she'd ever met.

Will Santo discover Fia's secret?

Find out in THE FORBIDDEN FERRARA
by USA TODAY bestselling author Sarah Morgan,
available this June from Harlequin Presents®!